AF243704

RESERVED FOR

TRAVELLING SHOWS

RESERVED FOR

TRAVELLING SHOWS

TRENT JAMIESON

PRIME BOOKS

RESERVED FOR TRAVELLING SHOWS
Copyright © 2006 by Trent Jamieson.
Cover art copyright © 2006 by Hawk Alfredson.
Cover design copyright © 2006 by Garry Nurrish.

ACKNOWLEDGEMENTS: A big thanks to Marianne de Pierres, Rowena Cory Daniells, Lyn Uhlmann, and Chris McMahon, the Unstoppable Thursday critiquers. Thanks also to Geoffrey Maloney for talking me into doing this. And of course the VISION writers group, Brisbane. Finally a HUGE thanks to all the wonderful (foolish) editors who've sustained me these past ten years, particularly, though in no real order, Jeremy G Byrne, Richard Scriven and Jonathan Strahan at Eidolon for being the first, to Robert Stephenson for picking a story at the right time, Cat Sparks for cutting through Gordian knots, Keith Stephenson for his excellent taste, Ben Payne Potato Monkey extraordinaire, and Ion Newcombe master Antipodean. Editors make the words go round.

for Diana—always

Prime Books
www.prime-books.com

CONTENTS

RESERVED FOR
TRULY GIFTED SOULS

There is no beginning, nor end, just consciousness skimming across eternity sealing up each moment and putting it in its place.—"Girl in a Black Dress."

Meet Trent Jamieson. He resides in omygod, a place reserved for a handful of truly gifted souls. In omygod Trent pens a seductive blend of fiction comprised of soaring ideas and romanticism—prose strewn with diamond dust and tasting of starwine.

Voyage with him into the worlds of A Woman in a Pool of Light in a Quantum Universe Smokes a Cigarette, Tar Baby, Carousel, My Brother is God, Threnody, Girl in a Black Dress and Always. Let these stories raze your worldview and reconstruct it with thoughtfulness and love. Let the tender, often melancholy, language flow around and inside you. Be changed by it.

Trent and I began a sporadic correspondence before finally meeting at an early Vision writers group meeting in Brisbane, Queensland in 1997. My first impression was of a serious, gentle person who possessed a startling facility with words. Over time, I've come to know his other facets—his self-deprecating, sardonic humour; his passion for his wife and muse, Diana; his genuine, all weather friendship and his kindness.

Over the last few years his work as a bookseller and as editor of the acclaimed dark fantasy magazine, *Redsine*, has only served to enhance his unique writing talent. *Reserved for Travelling Shows* is Trent's selection from over fifty of his published stories. These works have appeared in magazines all over the world including *Eidolon, Aurealis, Nowa Fantastyka* and the *Agog!* Press anthologies. To have them now in one collection is simply a reader's festival.

Celebrate!
Marianne de Pierres, 2006

THRENODY

They waited for her on the outskirts of town, smiling wanly at her approach, waving as she came down out of the hinterland. She saw them and waved back, before wiping away the sweat that had run onto her brow, blinking it out of her eyes. She walked slowly, picking her way through the rubble, the broken scab of the black and steaming road, hidden in places by thickweed and lantana. Her steps were careful, yet confident. The sun sat heavy in the sky and shadows had become mean little things incapable of solace—drought shadows, dead shadows.

But she was prepared, had travelled so many roads, and the failure of shade was not enough to bring her pause.

The wide-brimmed leather hat she wore was brittle and old, the face beneath it weathered, though young. Young as anything was these days.

"Hello, Threnodist," one of the townspeople called, when she was near enough to hear with ease. He was a man, tall and bulky, his wide face shadowed beneath his hat, his belly encased in taut flannelette.

She smiled and it was a weary thing.

"My name is Sal. Please call me that," she said and the man grinned back at her.

"As you wish, Threnodist. You heard our call and we are pleased."

"I hear all calls. I come when I can. What is this place named?"

"Alst, this place is . . . A tidy town, please wear your seat-belt."

"Alst, yes, I have heard of it." She smiled a little vaguely and glanced eastward.

The man was pleased, his head nodding, eyes flicking to the others. *She knows of us, see. Others know of this place.*

"Come now, out of this sun. We have lodgings for you and food and drink. And talk, you must hear our story. Know our lives and . . . "

"I know my job, man." She snapped. The man's eyes widened, a little stupidly, then he grinned. He grinned a lot; his face was creased with smiles.

"Of course, of course. I have a name too, " he said and reached out a hand. "William. I am the Speaker and the Caller. I called you here. We all have our roles, eh? All of us." She took his hand, her grip sure and strong, her dry hand surrounded by a sweaty palm and thick, sweaty fingers.

"That we do, William. That we do."

The little group walked down into the village and the day moved on.

* * *

Threnodists sing sad songs; sing for the dead, sing of the times before. They are the Travellers, those few who journey from village to village, that risk the bitter sun and their tenuous place upon the earth and learn and live beyond the outskirts.

They wait for the Call, then come.

A young one had died at this village; she felt the grief. The child had been much loved. Now he was no more. She would sing his song and he would be remembered. Perhaps the grief would be lessened then; not gone but made less bad. The ache softened. That was her role.

They left her alone to eat. Well, almost alone; a woman sat with her, young and sad and nervous. Sal found her pleasing to the eye and did not mind the company. Her name was Tine; she was William's woman, something Sal could see embarrassed her.

"There are too few men in this world," she had said to Sal, not moments after William had left the room, her face sullen and perhaps a little scornful. "Too few that I would have to settle for him."

Sal merely nodded and continued eating, sitting on the bed, hat off, resting now away from the sun; enjoying the fresh sandwiches that they had made for her. The mattress was firm and the sheets clean. Such comfort was rare.

A Traveller's life is hard; the road chews flesh, slow and steady. It makes you old. Sal felt old today, next to this sullen, pink cheeked woman. Older than she had felt in a long time. She laughed, softly, mockingly, at her self pity. She was still strong, not yet past her thirtieth summer. There were many years ahead. The laughter died then . . . many years.

"They say the sea is near here. Is that true?" Sal asked.

Tine nodded. "It is not far away; a day's easy walk, down the hills. The road has worn well that way."

"I like the sea," Sal said. "I have not been this close to Mother Water for so long."

Their eyes met, locked electric. Sal looked away. Tine's skin was pale, perfectly fair, her hair long and ginger. She would rarely travel outside unless clothed completely, face covered, skin covered. The sun ruined alabaster, tore at it with malign teeth.

"The sea wasps are in season now. It is not a good time for swimming."

"That is how the child died, wasn't it? Wasp sting?" Sal asked.

"He should have known better. It was a hot day. He had gone to the sea with the other boys. They all swam, only he was stung. When the body reached here it was a swollen thing long dead. The poison, the heat. All he had wanted was a swim, a little adventure and . . . but that is not my task. Others must tell you this."

"No," Sal said. "A Threnodist collects tales from all, draws all sadness. When the young die it is sorrow. There are so few, so few of any to fill the Long Wide Lands. Silence is the new dream now."

"Who draws the Threnodist's sorrow?" Tine asked and gently stroked her hair. She had come up close; Sal could feel her breath, warm and soft, against her cheek. Gently, she pushed her away, her pulse quickening, her face forced grim.

"No one. We cry alone."

"And why do you cry?"

Sal smiled, though her eyes were sad.

"We see the larger picture."

* * *

The boy's father saw her first. His face creased with a grief made hard, his hands rolled to balls, to spring open and shut, open and shut.

"He was a fool. Stupid, stupid child. This is wasp season. It has always been so." No not always; nothing is always, they all know that. "He should not have gone down there. I should have known he would—I should have . . . stupid, stupid boy." His voice cracked with bitterness. His jaw moved tight and straight. One eyelid flickered. His hands kept their steady rhythm of clenching and release. "Who is there to help in the fields now? My other sons are lazy things. They laugh at me, sometimes, think I am a fool old man, set in his ways. The soil is a gift, see. A blessing thing; from the earth comes life. But it must be nurtured, must be loved.

"They don't understand. They just don't understand. You've got to work to grow good crops; the sun is a cruel and jealous creature: burns the skin, burns the soil. You've got to work. Who is there now to help? Stupid . . . "

He stopped, embarrassed by his grief, eyes flicking away from this stranger.

"Threnodist, my son is dead. Sing of that. My son is dead."

He turned and walked away.

So they all came, one by one, spoke of the boy, of themselves, of their pain. Said what they would, said what they needed to say. What perhaps they couldn't have said to anyone but a stranger.

I didn't like him, never liked him, thought he was too brash. Too happy with his own thoughts. A trouble-maker, that's what he was, a trouble-maker. But I didn't want him to die. Never wanted him to die. You understand, I never wanted him to die. Never.

It took a day, long and hot and full of sad talk and happy memories. And when that day was over, and all had come who had wanted to come or were willing to come, she supped of their sadness, drew it into her, held it softly in her core until she knew that half her job was done. Now would come the song, but first she went to William, found him in his modest little home, reading a book.

Tine, her blue eyes wild, greeted her at the door. Somehow she knew what Sal would request. Tine's grin was open and warm. She said nothing, did not need to. Sal felt her pleasure.

William looked up from his book and smiled obsequiously.

"What is it that you need?" he asked her.

"Tomorrow, I want to go to the sea. I shall return the next day and that evening sing."

William frowned.

"Why not sing now? Most Threnodists . . . "

"I am not, "Most Threnodists". I will sing for this boy and his song will do what it must, but I need time. I will go to the sea, listen to its song, listen to what it has to say on the matter."

"Then you shall need a guide."

"I will take her," Tine said and smiled an almost hungry smile.

Sal nodded, suppressing a shiver. "She will do well."

"Yes," William reluctantly agreed. "Yes, she will."

* * *

They left in the early morning, the sun still a dim promise in the east, the villagers stirring or preparing to work. Occasionally an echidna would scurry before them, or a roo, surprised by this early morning human presence, would bound away into the scrub that lined the road. Magpies made deliquescent morning song and watched with beady, curious eyes these travellers passing by.

The day moved slowly as they followed the road to the sea. This road, reasonably well travelled, had been cared for. Vegetation did not press too close on either side and there were signs of lantana having been cut back and cleared. Still, none had the old skills with tar and stone, and in places huge swathes of road had slipped away, the hollows filled with grass.

Not far along the road, just beyond the next valley where two massive ridged and reaching fig trees grew, Tine stopped and motioned Sal to do so.

"Why are we stopping?" Sal asked, noticing Tine's eyes alive with excitement.

"We are near the spider place. Their webs are beautiful; it would be a pity to disturb them," she laughed. "They used to frighten me as a child. The webs are strong and sticky and apt to cling to your face, with a spider scurrying on your shoulder to send you screaming with fright. Now I see them for what they are."

"And what is that?" Sal asked.

"Beauty," Tine answered. "Unless, that is, you're an insect. And even then, even then . . ."

They walked on and came to a narrowing in the road, lined on either side by thick bushes, and there, dew-dropped golden, were the webs. Spiders, long legged with narrow, white-crossed bodies hung, still amongst the gleaming jewel-nested webs, or scurried to snare some insect stopped sudden in gold.

"Saint Andrew's cross," Sal said, as they ducked and weaved to avoid breaking the webs.

"What?" Tine asked.

"They are called Saint Andrew's Cross spiders."

"That's in the old tongue, isn't it?" Tine said, and Sal nodded.

"A clumsy language for speaking."

"Things were clumsy then, or so I have been told. The world was smaller; too much racing too little thinking. Clumsy languages suited such a place," she sighed. "The greatest irony, of course, is that now the opposite has happened. The world is bigger; slow thoughts are drowned in vastness. Our minds touch but we can grow lonely finding someone to reach."

"Are you lonely?" Tine asked. Sal eyed the webs thoughtfully then looked to her friend.

"Yes, I suppose I am. I have travelled far, Tine. Very far. I have been a traveller as long as I can remember, with my father first; a teacher he was, then a Threnodist, who took me on as an apprentice, said I had a lovely voice. But more, he said I sang from the gut." She laughed softly. "All Threnodists must do that, Tine. The gut is the truth and the strength of it all. Sing the truth and sing it strong and it *will* touch others."

"Sing for me," Tine said.

And Sal sang.

* * *

It was almost evening by the time they made it to the beach, waves singing their steady song and roar, patient devourers of land. An empty village ran right into the sea. It waited, weary and broken, for time and nature's rage to tear it ungentle from the face of the earth. And slowly, undeniably, that was happening. It was less a village now than a suggestion of a village that once had been.

They stopped for a while in the thickening shadows to gather wood for a fire.

Sal saw old cars, rust-withered and twisted but still recognizable as what they had once been. Out on the dry plains she had come across such things, by the roadside and in far better condition; still, she marvelled at them. Around her neck she wore a large bead of glass that enclosed a single H. All Travellers wore such things as charms; hers, she knew, was particularly powerful. Cars had once made travelling much, much easier; still, there had been too many of them. The road to The Changing had been an easy one, ridden in the bellies of such vehicles; a swift and reckless drive in a world grown too small. They all knew that.

The cars were broken, though they made good trinkets for Travellers and the like, and the world was once more huge.

Tine, who knew which houses still had good, salvageable wood and weren't too overgrown with grumblegrass and lantana to reach, led the way. She talked as she went, speaking quick and warm of things past and things yet to come.

"No one lives here now. This place is lonely; ghosts haunt it. Sad things they are, flitting things, fearful and cold. There is no rest here anymore, just the wind to fill the mind and deny it sleep. We will not stay here." She snatched up pieces of wood, dry and perfect for burning, and handed them to Sal. When Sal's hands were full, as were her own, they moved from the village out across the beach, being careful to watch for any wasps that might have drifted ashore on the tide. Flaccid now and withered but still deadly if touched.

They found a hollow in the dunes, a little away from the high tide. It had obviously been used many times before. Large, well worn rocks for sitting on circled a fire pit.

Sal stretched a blanket on the sand and watched Tine set the fire. She moved with lithe precision, her face twisted in concentration, laying the wood carefully, then lighting the tinder with quick, sure strokes. Her movements practised, Sal was sure: both economical and erotic, her hips swaying smooth.

The fire was blazing quickly, more a vanity than a need on this warm summer's night. Shadows danced and flared trails over their faces, softening hard lines, melting time, bringing out beauty.

Sal stared out at the black mass of the sea, delighting in the soft bite of its breath; its constant, soothing rumble. A wind blowing in from the north tangled and played with her hair. It's been so long, she thought, so very long. For a while at least, the excitement, the knowing, the nearness to Tine's pale beauty slipped from her, her soul flooded in static, insistent waves of night and seaside roar.

"This place relaxes me," she said. "I feel at home here."

Tine nodded.

"We all do," she said. "The sea calls us, doesn't she: Return to me, return."

"Did he hear her cry?" Sal mused aloud. "Or was it just his blood that called, fiercest echo of the sea, crying, pulsing in his veins. Tine, oh Tine, why do we do such foolish things?"

Tine looked thoughtful and Sal found herself loving her for it, loving the strength of her face in the shadows, loving the way she held her head and hands.

"Sometimes it's because we must and sometimes because we can't return."

Sal thought then of the boy and the sea, the indifferent, empty sea. The pleasure of it all faded away, slipped out her grasp till only darkness remained.

"I have no home," she said and wept. "I am tired and lonely. Too much grief; there is too much grief."

Tine came then and held her. The tears stopped at last, ran themselves dry into the evening, brushed away by Tine's soft lips, the warm touch of her breath.

They made love.

*　*　*

They awoke to light rain and slate grey sky. They nuzzled and kissed, wanting no end to it all but knowing that it would. All things end. Some things last but a single evening and dawn; held then released.

They ate a quick breakfast, dried meat and fruit, detachment already building between them, reality a gulf to widen with each passing moment. The Threnodist felt sad, her belly tight. She laughed bitterly and Tine watched her, seeming to understand but distant all the same. She was sated, had had her fill without the lonely miles between. Sal resented her that.

Threnodists are sadness: incarnations of grief, to draw and sing, black strands in the ragged web that is humanity. It is their job. They are called, they come. And what happens after . . .

Tine reached out and gripped Sal's shoulders. As always the touch was gentle, yet electric.

"It was nice," she said.

Sal pulled away, thinking: *Is that all you can say? Nice; just nice.*

"Yes it was," she said.

And they walked back to the Village of Alst.

At the outskirts of the village lands, alone and in the darkening shadows, Tine held her.

Sal smiled, enjoying this last, true display of affection before speaking.

"I am leaving tonight," she said. "It is my way. After the song

I must leave: I cannot stay and spoil what little magic the song will hold. Threnodists are travellers: we do our job then go."

Tine nodded her head.

"I will meet you tonight, then, once you have sung. I *will* say goodbye," she said. "Wait for me."

* * *

Sal sang her song, his song, their song, the song of pain and past, and they listened and wept or stood silent and sad in the hall where most times there were (and would be) dances and jauntier music but now there was only grief and the single, pale thread of her threnody. Her voice was beautiful, the song was beautiful, words and feelings traced it, danced within each other, rose above the still summer night and echoed amongst the stars.

Afterwards, she packed her meagre belongings and made to leave, despite their wishes that she stay, another day, another night. The boy's mother clung to her; she was their daughter now, would always be their daughter. *Stay, stay.* But Sal remained resolute in her leaving. The boy was gone, the song sung. Both were memories.

William led her from the village.

"You sang well," he said. "You sang very well, perhaps the best Threnodist that we have ever had. I am pleased you heard our call. Well pleased."

Sal merely nodded. Then William said something that surprised her.

"My wife, she slept with you, did she not? She does it with all Travellers." William, seeing her stiffen, did not wait for any other answer. "It is her way. I am not enough, I have never been enough. She has always needed more. There, that is my grief. Take it please.

"We all have our needs, Threnodist. All of us. All have that which must be released. You realise this, of course, you who are well-travelled."

His face was a shadow in the soft wall of night, impenetrable. Still, she thought she detected a smile.

"You sang well."

He turned, then was gone, back to the light and people and the tears now shed. Sal waited some time but no one came. After a while she sighed, chuckled softly, bitterness scarcely detectable in the sound, and threaded her way into the night.

Walked alone, a shadow amongst shadows, waiting for the call; and when it came it was far away and nowhere near the sea.

Walked alone; and when the call came she answered with her song, as was the way in the Long Wide Lands.

A Traveller, she walked alone.

ALWAYS

My work, my driving work, was done.

We had pierced the shivering membrane of the universe, and the last Way Station was already so distant that it defied imagination.

Standard procedure.

I can drive here, as my licence will attest. I've earned the right and the bitter nugget of pride that comes with it; regardless it's something that's better off left to the AI. Safer.

But it's not just a driving job; it's a people one, too.

These passengers were my wards.

"You gotta love them. Love them honestly," Govinda once told me, long ago. "Every single one of them needs you more than they can ever know."

I was taking them off world, between worlds; across a lot of space and a lot of time. You take the Highway and there's no going back.

For driver and passenger both.

After Deb died, I took up this job, started running and haven't stopped. When you lose your Everything, driving doesn't look like such a bad deal.

"We're all wounded here," Govinda said, when she started my training. "You've just gotta accept it. Gotta work with it."

Govinda was one of the best, she taught me at the end of her career. But then, careers do not end here; they ripple. You do not leave the highway, not really, there's always echoes. I've come across her several times since, at Way Station bars and the like, but they all predate me.

None of them know of the single night we shared late in my training. An evening that stripped away a little of the pain, or, maybe, made it something else. Because after that night I'd fled her too, drove away into a different place and time.

The only thing worse was the one time I saw myself. An earlier me, driving my first bus, a big and basic model. It hurt, catching a glimpse of my past; certain brutal truths were driven home.

I was sadder, angrier, still struggling with responsibilities that I hadn't even considered would come with the job. Well, that was how I remember it.

But damned if I could see that in my eyes. Because the truth is I don't remember what I was thinking back then. Hell, even if I did, it would be an illusion distorted by the years that separated us, by the things that I have learnt and seen, by the endless mutable miles of the Highway.

I saw the blank incomprehensible face that was my own and realised that time had severed me from my past. Now. Everything is *now*, perpetually changing, merely coated with a crust of apparent stability. The me on the tip of the wave.

I hid before I could see myself. It's little wonder that few search themselves out at the Way Stations, or look too closely at rigs that could be their own.

No one likes to see their own face and the stranger behind it.

* * *

I got up from the driver's—and, after a cursory glance at the monitors—everything sitting green and clean—I looked over my passengers.

This is the transportation of the lost. There are other, faster, ways and some that eschew corporality altogether, but none are cheaper than the buses.

However, these travellers must pay in other ways.

The Highways distort time, they are unshielded from relativity or, as some arguments go, extremely susceptible to it. You can end up at a depot a thousand years before you began, or a hundred thousand years after. Something to do with Temporal-Spatial Flex. I've never understood the physics and if anyone asks I can rattle out the TSF ratios and the standard company spiel, but that's where my knowledge ends. I just drive the bus and help my passengers make it through.

What it all boils downs to is this, you pay your money and you take your chances.

If there is any continuity in the universe, I have yet to find evidence of it, beyond pain and the Highways. Beyond the road that stretches on forever and the past that drives you along it.

* * *

There were about forty passengers on the bus—thirty of these tuned out—plugged in to whatever personal systems they could afford. The usual stuff, VR simulators, powder fabulators, even a couple of straight-up personal sound systems of the sort you slip into your ears rather than your cortex.

I walked the length of the bus and those who hadn't zoned out clung to me with their eyes. I chatted and calmed, dipped into the all too large collection of lame jokes that I knew, and did my best to take their minds off what was happening. Every single one of them would have fretted enough. You do not make this decision lightly; they deserved a break from their doubts.

Among them was a girl in a bright floral dress. She didn't have any personal entertainment systems, not even a simple stereo unit. Sara Edwards. You know all their names, that's part of the job. I'd packed her things in a side compartment. Her luggage was small, almost pathetically light, though the nervous smile that she gave me was weighted with so much hope.

"Do you think it will be a long journey?"

I shook my head.

"There's no way of knowing, Sara. The times chop and change. Often it takes thirty hours, others we're there in under ten."

She gripped my arm, gently but firmly, and I noticed the bruises, poorly hidden by make-up running from her wrists to her shoulder. Sara's chin, too, bore the faintest memory of a bruise.

"I hope it doesn't take too long." Her gaze flicked to the window. "It's weird out there. I'd read about the Highways of course, everything I could find, but I didn't expect it to be so . . . unsettling."

I smiled my most professional and calming smile. "It can be beautiful. The things I've seen, some of them can take your breath away."

But the dust that beat against the glass then was nothing special. Just the usual spiral of light, the active charge of the bus wasn't disturbing the particles all that much which meant the TS Flux cycle was in a quiescent phase.

Still, I knew what she meant; I'd felt the same way. It's the physics of it all, the mind-bending paradox of the Highway. It spans the universe, but should not be. The greatest alien artefact—if it is indeed an artefact at all or, for that matter, alien—and we drive buses along it.

That's the human species for you. Give us all the wonders in the universe and we'll find a way to make them mundane.

"How long have you been doing this?" she asked

I looked down at her. My face twisted. I could feel it, an involuntary reaction that I'd never quite been able to outrun. "A long time. A long, long time."

Leaving Sara to her thoughts, I walked to the toilets. Gareth had gleefully informed me of the mess waiting down there. Someone had thrown up, missing the bowl and spraying over the floor. The acrid smell of vomit, not at all an unfamiliar one on these journeys, clung to the back of my throat. The cleaning module on my bus was running on one third efficiency—I hoped to get it fixed at the next Way Station—but that didn't help me now.

Sighing, I reached for the old-fashioned mop and bucket and got to work.

"There's something up ahead," Gareth subbed, just as I finished.

"What exactly?"

There was a moment of almost exasperated silence.

"If I knew I would tell you. I don't trade in ambiguities. It's some kind of distortion on the road. I could run over it, but I think we should stop."

I walked up front. Buses are almost indestructible, self-repairing, and very cautious. There is little room for error out here.

"Okay, let's do it."

Gareth stopped the bus about a hundred meters from the anomaly, the dust died down. He launched one of his drones to take a look.

"It's a face," Gareth said. Then brought the image up on the cockpit monitor.

I went cold. "I'm going out there."

"Are you sure that's wise?"

"Deb," I whispered. "That's Deb's face."

* * *

I slipped on the armour and felt it mould around my body. I avoided the mirror instinctively. I knew I cut a fairly ridiculous figure; a tin man with a round belly. Too much driving and not enough exercise or vanity to pay for fat-eating viruses. I used to be vain, not any more.

Deb would have laughed at me and the thought of her, not to mention the thought of what lay out there, sent a chill down my spine.

The passengers were all staring at me now, and I lifted the faceplate and smiled.

"I'm sorry about this. There's something on the road and I am going to have to look at it before we can go on. It's standard procedure." I hoped my face wasn't too pale. My hands were numb in the cool containment of the armour. It certainly didn't feel like standard procedure.

"What if something happens to you out there?" Sara asked.

"If something happens to me, Gareth will take over. But nothing will happen. The external atmosphere is within standard parameters. There has never been any trouble on the Highway, and there's absolutely no reason to expect it now."

Of course, none of that was absolutely true. You drive long enough and you hear stories—things on the road, buses coming in empty, their AI's memory wiped clean—never from someone who's actually experienced them, never often enough to give credence to the tales, just enough to plant a seed of doubt. Something was out there and the armour, more a shield against the radiation that the TSF occasionally generated, felt completely inadequate.

I stepped through the door and it shut behind me with a click.

I walked towards the anomaly, my breathing loud in my ears.

"Your heart rate is up a little," Gareth said.

"What do you expect?"

"There, I've fixed it."

I thought about Deb. Her death was swift, a freak accident. There had been a sudden depressurisation of the skytube she and her schoolchildren were taking, the result of a flaw in the spun-diamond walls of the tube and a micro-meteor impact.

Seventy-one people died in seconds, the oxygen in their blood boiling away. Deb had always said she would try and contact me if she died first and, in a way, she had.

Somehow she had managed a simple text message. I found it in my log a day after the accident. One word.

always.

* * *

That word was in my head as I walked along the highway. Towards a replica of her face.

At last I reached the spot and looked down. I felt as though someone had punched me. I forgot to breathe. Deb. She was as beautiful as I remembered. That's it with faces, you think you forget, that they've faded from all hope of true recollection, and then it burns back, perfect. And with that single image comes a flood of emotions, of memories, little things you didn't realise that you had ever noticed, the small scar under her right ear, the wry curl of her lips.

I gazed upon her features and tears splashed against my faceplate.

It was surreal, almost Daliesque. Where the road ended was Deb's skin, pale and freckled as I remembered her skin to be.

"Is that really flesh?" I asked.

"No," Gareth replied. "It *is* remarkably lifelike, but it's definitely not flesh."

I crouched down to touch it, and the face opened its eyes.

Deb's bright green eyes stared at me and I stumbled back.

"Richard?" She said and then the face was gone, swallowed up by the road.

I fell to my knees, and scrambled to the spot where it had been. Gone. I clawed my gloved fingers over the road and wept.

* * *

Deb gave me a piece of rose quartz on our second date and it is all I keep of her. That and her final message. Sometimes when I am at my darkest. I open that e-mail.

always.

I sat in the cockpit and watched the universe smudge against the glass. The quartz felt soft in my hand. I squeezed it until my fingers ached.

"What was out there?" Sara asked, surprising me, so that I almost dropped the stone.

"Just the ghost of a memory," I said.

She smiled.

"Sometimes I wish I could remove all my memories. Just wipe the slate clean."

"They fade eventually. Every memory fades."

"Do they?" she said. "I think memories are always. I think we spend our lives circling around them, trying to give them meaning."

I stared out at the road, the dust was growing more excitable, charged particles dancing like ghosts around the bus.

"I loved her and now she is gone."

Sara squeezed my shoulder.

"I loved him and he beat me up. Beat me and yet I loved him so much. Even now I feel I betrayed him. At least your memories are good."

She left me then and walked back to her seat.

"There's another anomaly coming up," Gareth said.

I took a deep breath.

"Stop when you're close. I'm going out again."

* * *

The hand was curled into a fist, rising out of the road. I reached down and it grabbed me. The grip was strong enough that I could feel it through the armour. Reflexively, I pulled back, engines in the suit whined, monitors went red, but I did not give up and the hand rose.

It came with an arm, then a head and shoulders. I fell to the ground—Gareth yelling in my skull.

Deb looked down at me and blinked. She was still holding my hand, slowly she pulled me to my feet.

"Richard," she said. "It's coming."

I shook my head. "What's coming?"

"You'll know when it arrives. I know I shouldn't but . . . "

Something caught her attention behind me. Her eyes widened and then she was gone, collapsed back into the road.

I turned but there was nothing there. Nothing at all.

* * *

"If it is at all reassuring, I cannot detect any other anomalies."

"Thanks, Gareth," I said. "But I don't know what we're dealing with. Deb, she, whatever she was, spoke to me."

"I know," Gareth said. "It may have looked like Deb, but it wasn't human."

"What was it then?" I asked.

"The road, it was the same substance as the road."

Which meant that Gareth didn't have a clue. No one did.

We were travelling down the Highway at around seven hundred kilometres an hour—twice the usual speed. Both Gareth and I agreed that if we could avoid running into whatever was coming all the better. Outside the dust in the void had become increasingly agitated—mad patterns spiralled against the glass.

I looked back at my passengers, they seemed more than a little agitated too. Someone was throwing up in the toilets—I hoped they had better aim than the last person. I would have to speak to them all soon.

A beeper went off in the cockpit and I smiled.

The nearest exit had locked onto us, we'd be off the Highway in under two hours.

A storm was coming, but with any luck we would miss us entirely.

* * *

"Um, Richard. We appear to be having a problem. Something is slowing the bus down. Everything is working properly and yet there's a measurable reduction in speed." Gareth sounded worried. "Richard, I don't know if I can trust my sensors any more."

I nodded, understanding his fears. AI's are all sensors and readings. If they lose the ability to understand them, they lose the ability to function.

"I think you should take over here," Gareth said. "I need to concentrate on making some sense of all this."

"Okay, I'll switch to manual." The bus was suddenly under my control, the sheer power of it rumbling into my hands through the steering wheel. We were definitely still moving, though according to Gareth we were not.

I pushed the speed up to 900.

"Richard, we're going backwards."

"What!"

I pulled the bus to a halt. Then I felt it, a slight shuddering in the wheel. A sense of something building.

"It's coming," I whispered and got to my feet.

* * *

I opened the door and looked out, nothing. No movement.

"How fast are we going?"

"Fast, very fast and it's increasing exponentially. We'll reach light speed in around two minutes."

I began to wonder why we weren't dead. The acceleration should have crushed us. The armour I wore suddenly felt very insignificant. I looked at my passengers and they looked at me, everybody was most definitely switched on.

"Something is happening," I said. "But I'm going to do whatever I can to get you through this."

"It's coming," Sara said, gripping the hem of her dress tightly in her hands then releasing. "It's here."

Something slammed into us, the bus creaked and Gareth shrieked with it, then shut down. I was thrown to the floor, a couple of passengers hit their heads and then, there was silence.

Only for a moment. We looked at each other.

Voices, there were hundreds of voices, thousands, millions, billions upon billions and I realised suddenly they had always been there, a kind of background radiation of chatter. Always there, but never really noticed, maybe I hadn't known how to listen.

"Gareth," I subbed. "What's happening?"

There was no response, no static, no sense of Gareth's presence at all. It chilled me to the bone. Nothing to give me data updates, or slow a racing heart. I walked up and down the aisle, but for a few bruised heads everybody seemed okay

"I want you all to stay inside," I said, then walked to the door, opened it, and my jaw dropped.

The road was gone, replaced by faces, a concretation of expressions stretching away into the distance.

I jumped from the bus and they parted before me, creating a path leading away from the bus, leading towards Deb. My head spun, what was going on?

Cautiously, I walked towards her. And when, at last, we stood face to face, she hugged me, tightly.

"Rich, you've been running a long time. A very long time. I can't believe that it took so long to catch up."

"Not that long, surely," I said. "Years maybe, but not that long."

She brought a finger to my lips. "Longer than you think, Rich. Longer than you suspect." She squeezed my hand. "There's someone I think you might want to see."

Govinda smiled at me as we approached.

"Richard, get out of that armour. You don't need it here."

I nodded and, as I stripped out of the intelligent metal, I looked along the road at that highway of faces, every eye trained on me.

"What's happening?" I asked. "What the hell's going on? I've got passengers back there."

"Those passengers are your wards, Richard. And you've always looked after them well, but who looks after you?"

"I don't need looking after."

Govinda laughed and Deb with her; these two women whom I'd loved and lost.

"That may be right," Govinda said. "But you've been hurting for a long time. You've been driving for such a long time."

"No longer than anyone else," I said, knowing it was a lie. "And I've never needed help. I get my passengers to their destination, I make sure that they're all right and then I take the next load on."

"When was the last time you got off the Highway?"

I realised I couldn't answer that. The truth is you never stop when you're driving. There's always more people to take a little further up the road. God, I couldn't remember when I'd last stopped for more than a day at a Way Station.

"Is that all you've stopped me for, to tell me that I need to relax?"

Govinda laughed. "You were always thickheaded, Richard. Kind heart, thick head. *You've* been calling us. A hundred years, a thousand. Why, you've been calling us since the beginning of time."

"What do you think this road is? How do you think it works? The Highway is as ancient as that first eternal instant, when the galaxies, the clumping pulsing fire of it all, were put into place. When heat was beyond heat when the universe itself paused before its first great inflationary burst."

"And you've been calling us since then." Govinda laughed.

"Took a long while to catch up. But then you never stopped, Rich."

I looked at Deb. My Deb.

"Always," she whispered. "The Universe is always."

And I hung my head and wept.

"I've missed you, Rich. You never let me go. But you have to. The more you run, the more it just builds up behind you." I felt her fingers on my face.

"You died," I said. "And I couldn't do a thing. What was I supposed to do? You died and I couldn't change it. Couldn't fix it."

Deb brushed my face with her fingers.

"The only thing you could fix was yourself, Rich. Get on with your life. Now let me go."

I lifted my gaze to hers and knew that I would never see it again. Not so perfectly.

She smiled.

"Heal yourself, Rich."

"I miss you."

Deb smiled.

"I wouldn't expect it any other way."

Then she was gone.

I turned to Govinda. "What do you want?" I asked and she smiled sadly.

"Honey, this isn't about what I want. It's about what you *need*. You don't stop running until you're ready." She looked at me. The highway looked at me, with its multitude of eyes. "Are you ready?"

"My passengers . . . "

Then I felt a familiar presence in my skull.

"Rich," Gareth said. "Back online. There's some serious Flux work here, and I think it's going to get even more interesting." Gareth paused, reading something in my expression or remembering, then said softly, "I can take them on."

"Gotta talk to them first," I said.

Slowly I walked back to the bus.

They were frightened; I could see it in their eyes. But I was frightened too. I'd felt this storm behind me for longer than I knew, perhaps ever since I got on the road.

So I smiled and it relaxed them a little.

I told them what Govinda had told me. Told them how I'd been running for so long. I apologised and they forgave me.

"Sometimes you've just got to leave," I said. "Some day that's all you can do."

"I'll look after them," Gareth said. "It's what I was made for. Maybe I'll see you sometime."

"Yeah," I said.

Sara gripped my hand, face resolute.

"I'm coming with you too."

I looked into her eyes and knew that she meant it.

"Okay," I said, not knowing what else to say, just that it felt right.

I walked towards the baggage compartment to get her things and she stopped me.

"I don't think we'll need that where we're going."

"Gareth," I said. "There's one more thing I'd like you to do."

"What's that?"

"Clear my inbox. I don't need it any more."

I picked up the quartz then put it down, I didn't need that any more, either. I could not forget her, she was as much a part of me as life itself. She had followed, down every road, down infinities beyond knowing.

"Sara, are you ready?"

"Yes, I think I am."

We stepped out of the bus, then watched it drive away and I felt not fear but relief. Govinda was waiting and behind her, not far away at all, the road was shifting, changing, a door taking shape. Our own private exit.

"Where are we going?" I asked

Govinda smiled, reaching for the door.

"This is the Highway, who can tell where or when. You pay your money and you take your chances. Why don't you walk through and find out."

I looked at Sara, and she held my gaze, then, hand in hand, that's what we did.

BOUNTY

Night, and the birds fell again, an avian rain.

Pin could hear the dead creatures smacking onto rooftops. No heavy drumming this time. After last night there could be few birds left. People had died, brained in the previous evening's downpour. The streets below were empty, the lamps untended. The Lamplighters' Guild had suffered terribly.

One blessing at least, with the city so dark, the sky was brighter than usual as Pin—his eye pressed hard against the cool ocular—focussed his telescope on the craggy old moon then the greater constellations. For all he knew they would be the next things to fall out of the sky.

Someone chuckled behind him. "Thought I might find you here, Wizard. Head in the clouds as the birds drop out of them."

Pin sighed.

"Sendle, the answer lies up there. I am sure of it."

The king's Man-at-arms and executioner—he called it chopping wood—leant against the battlements and pointed down. "The people grow nervous. But they are always nervous. Portents are always grim. Still this *is* disquieting. Even for a man like me.

"You know, there used to be a forest out there. My family cut it down. Every single last tree."

"Yes, you did a good job," Pin said, teeth clenched.

Sendle laughed.

"If there is one thing I know it is how to chop wood. A kingdom is much like a forest, Pin. It must be cared for, part of it must be culled. Get rid of the dead wood, the vermin and rot, and the forest thrives."

"But not that forest, eh?" Pin stared down into the city.

Sendle jovially slapped him upon the back, jolting his spine, and Pin silently cursed his odd confidant.

"But there are other forests. There always are, and look at the wonder we built on the tomb of the old."

A bird fell at their feet, startling them both. Pin looked down at the broken-necked thing. His face twisted with disgust as he bent to pick it up. Its lifeless bones shifted beneath his fingers. Its air chambers let out a last, meaningless chirp.

"The sky is a tomb now. And what can we build on that?"

* * *

Pin's room, despite its size, was cluttered. Live long enough and all you have is clutter, regrets and fears, stacked teetering on high. And Pin had lived a very long time.

He lit a half-dozen candles and, in their warm light, his machines and instruments glowed dully. In one corner, cups and plates piled up that would have been cleared away long ago if he ever let the servants into his chambers, cockroaches scurried from them and into the shadows.

He held the bird in one hand. It felt much lighter than it ought. As though with its life it had also lost a goodly portion of its weight, though its mass appeared the same. He dropped it on a work bench, brought out his scales and weighed the bird.

Far too light. Far too light. He gazed out a narrow slit of a window up at the stars. What was happening out there?

He left the bird where it was and walked to his library, more clutter for the most of it. He pulled a few of the older volumes, long unread, from the shelves.

Clutter. Clutter. Clutter.

No answer to be found here, surely. But amongst the dissertations on the corpuscularity of light and the shiftings of constellations, he found it, and was at once, violently and terribly sick.

* * *

King Catchincraw rubbed at his bleary eyes and stumbled up and down the chamber, looking for something to hit. "This cannot be. Entropy? The end of the world. I expected some sort of Avian disease, but this . . . "

Pin nodded, bones aching, his heart a pain in his chest, a dull but weakening ache.

"But it is. The aether contains a finite amount of force and we have consumed all but the last. Our days are run out."

Catchincraw scowled, and crashed a fist against the wall.

"This defies reason. It is Spring! The gardens bloom, the farmers are at harvest, and we are at peace."

Pin shook his head. "And The Wilt we have been hearing of? You seem to have neglected that. Local farms may be ready for harvest, but the edges of the kingdom, their crops are dying. People lie sick in their beds. I thought it the plague, but now I know otherwise." He paused and held his king's scared gaze. "Every flower, every breath is a drain in what are limited reserves. Life's bounty has become a curse. A day or two, no more, and then all that binds and drives our world will be used up."

Pin had taught this king, had raised him, even now he slipt into the role of lecturer, he paced the room, one finger in the air, an almost condescending expression washing across his angular face. "You see, the world will not end in fits and starts. But suddenly, like a wind-up toy when its dance is done."

"Well, can we not just wind it up again?"

Pin could not resist a wan smile. How quickly they slipped back into the old roles of pupil and student.

"Oh what Power we would need. More than was contained in our universe at its genesis. I do not have such magics at my disposal."

"So there is nothing we can do?" The King cleared the contents of a nearby shelf with an outflung hand. Glass and pottery shattered on the floor and with them were shattered Pin's illusions. "So we are dead? And so you tell me in such a calm voice. Well, perhaps dear Sendle should chop a little wood."

He reached for the wizard.

Pin ducked out of the way and, taking a deep breath, brought the glass staff out from under his robes. It gleamed in the candle-light, seemed to pull at it. The room was at once brighter and dimmer in its presence.

The King froze.

"What is that?"

Pin's hands shook.

"The one thing we can do."

* * *

"Are you sure this will work?"

How Pin hated that voice. His eyes flicked towards Sendle. The man was an animal, but after today, how could Pin count himself as any better.

"As sure as I can be of anything," Pin said. "What I am about to do breaks no natural laws, just cheats a little."

The King's axe-man laughed.

"Is that not the nature of magic? Tricks and cheats and smoke and mirrors. Perhaps, you will destroy us all. Have you given any thought to that?"

More than you could ever know.

Pin brought his horse to a halt, his mouth was dry and his hands shook slightly on the pommel of his saddle.

"Why are you here?"

"To see that you go through with it. To stop you. I don't know. I don't trust you, wizard."

Nor I you, Pin thought; though he smiled a tight-lipped smile and kept quiet. Pin wasn't sure if he trusted himself either.

Early morning and spring was caught on winter's chill memory. The city was not big, the road round its walls a good one, it would not take them long to circle it. He looked back at the city.

Not much to see in the near darkness; the suggestion of form; the odd geometries of rooftops; the thicker darkness of smoke. Lights burned in the grey bulk of the castle above. Night was still a great carcass that the worms of morning had scarce begun to nibble on.

But for Pin and Sendle, not a soul outside the keep was aware of what was about to happen. Pin was uncertain himself, and scared, very scared.

His horse shivered beneath him.

"Time to begin."

He took a deep breath and pulled the glass staff from the saddlebag, it sucked at his fingertips and, for a moment, all he wanted to do was hurl it away. Hurl it away and run. Instead he looked askance at Sendle.

"Dreadful magics and determination alone can save us," Pin said.

Sendle grinned like a wolf.

"And fear, wizard. Don't forget fear."

Fear, yes, plenty of fear.

* * *

The horses' hooves clattered (and crunched) loudly on the stony bird-littered road, but not as loudly as the spell roaring in his mind. A deep whispering of magic that had become vast and crushing. The staff burned his fingers, but he gripped it as though all life depended on it. Well, a little life, part of which was his own.

Sendle rode with him, quiet as a shadow.

Then, as sunlight breached the eastern hills, they completed the circuit of the city. The spell was a quickening ocean in his mind: tides and waves crashing on the shore of his consciousness.

Time and motion stilled. A grim and hungry expectation that lasted, perhaps a heartbeat but felt like an eternity.

Pin raised the staff above his head and let it do what it would.

The final words of his spell tumbled from him, drawn on by the engine of his magic, the vast inertial pull of this casting. Those last words, key words, binding words grew, just as they had grown in his mind, a whispering, then a shouting, then a booming; a raging storm that was word and magic and power.

And they consumed all.

The glass staff burned in his grip as though it would swallow him too.

Pin sensed movement, or, perhaps, some malevolent intent, behind him. He spun in his saddle and saw Sendle's eyes widen, saw shock and hate flower there, saw the executioner reach for his sword, then the callused fingers fall away to swing up and cover his eyes. Pin followed his broken gaze.

Beyond Pin's magical boundary the world collapsed. No that wasn't right. It simply evaporated. Colour, form and movement; hazing; shrinking; fading, drawn into the staff.

The last days of a whole world used to feed a single city.

Kingdoms old as humanity itself fall today, he thought.

The glass staff roared at its intaking of power, and flared with a cold light as bright as the sun. Pin's body was on fire, his skin prickled. A washed-out greyness rushed towards the horizon then beyond.

Pin looked down at his hands—colour had bled from them—then glanced at Sendle, colourless in nature now in truth.

"My eyes were brown," Pin said. "I must not forget that."

Sendle grunted and patted Pin's back companionably.

"We are alive, wizard."

* * *

That damned scraping. Why, oh why? Knife against fork. Scrape. Scrape.

He hadn't eaten in fifteen years.

Nor had anyone else in the city drowned in the sea of grey which he had created. And what was worse, fifteen years and he hadn't felt like eating.

There was no need.

The plates and cutlery were set in tradition's name alone. A few of the duller knights still thought it high wit to scrape their knives and forks across the vacant crockery.

He scowled at them; they ignored him. And because he found it hard to sustain passion or anger he let it pass, let it subside to a point where in perhaps another month or two it might drive him to momentary distraction.

"Fifteen years," Sendle said, somehow echoing his thoughts.

"Age does not weary us."

"Aye, it does not. Nothing changes." Sendle raised an empty goblet in toast, thick grey fingers clutching the goblet's gold stem—now the colour of slate. Pin's eyes narrowed.

"This place suits you doesn't it?"

"Wizard, I am alive."

"Indeed."

The king then motioned for silence and all around the hall the chatter—and scrapings—stopped.

"Bring it in," he said. "Bring it in."

Courtiers carried the kaleidoscope out on a pillow of silk and the hall hushed. Here alone was hunger. A page placed it by the king, who peered a while into the tube then passed it on.

Pin half made up his mind not to look, after all he had cast the thing and its sisters; tubes of spell negating silver and a spiralling interweave of glass and coloured beads.

But when it came to his turn he gazed at it as hungrily as the rest.

Only Sendle passed it on with not even a glance.

"The townsfolk will be getting their glimpse of colour tonight. Keeps them quiet, but what choice do they have?

"You have made a perfect system, dear wizard. Without colour, without taste, without hunger or age, what is there but control?"

Pin shook his head.

"I destroyed a world, Sendle."

"No, you saved a world." He raised his goblet high. "Not just saved. You created an even better one."

Pin grimaced and excused himself from the table.

* * *

The walk into town cleared his head, not much, but a little for everywhere was warm and still and grey. Evening had shadowed the streets, though it was barely perceptible. Even darkness was muted now. He could hear the town's festivities in the distance when another sound caught his attention. The low murmuring of voices in a nearby alley.

He followed the susurration to its source, and gasped at what he saw.

A child lay on his back, children were crouching round, poking and prodding with thin wooden rods at a hole in his skull.

"What are you doing?" Pin demanded.

The children took fright and ran.

The wizard crouched down and touched the boy's hand.

"Are you all right, child?"

The boy smiled.

"I am no more a child than you, Mr Pin. I am twenty-five years old, though my body is that of a ten year old. Stop treating us as children, stop giving us the kaleidoscope last. Do you know if you prod certain parts of the brain you can see colours?"

"Yes, but one wrong stab . . . "

The boy smiled.

"Wizard, I would welcome oblivion." He shoved the rod even deeper into his head.

"Yellow." He whispered as the seizures began, then bit off his tongue.

Pin carried the child to his parents.

"He will not die. But this is something worse, your child's mental damage is beyond repair."

The parents seemed more disturbed that they had missed their chance at the colour.

"The kaleidoscope will be brought out next month," Pin said. "This is forever."

"So are we," the boy's father said. "So are we. Can you not make more colour, Lord Pin? Can you not give us that?"

Pin stared at his slate hands.

"No, I cannot."

Like the colour, and his hunger, his powers were gone. Seven kaleidoscopes he'd made and he had no strength for more.

"Then perhaps he is the lucky one. Perhaps where he lives inside his head is a place of colours."

"I doubt it."

"But you do not know."

Pin turned from the man and ran. Of course, well before he reached the castle he had no real energy for it. He walked the last half mile slowly and by the time he reached the castle's gates he wept but only a little. It was all too much to cry.

* * *

Each night the dream was the same.

Death drew near, a dark and hungry creature. It trailed him down city streets where lights burned brightly until Pin ran past, his passage stilling flame and startling birds that would trace shaky parabolas as they rose into the air and plummeted moments later, dead. It whispered his name down alleyway and hall, until, in terror, Pin ran beyond the walls of the city, out into the fields or where there had once been fields.

And above, the stars shone bright and pure, though with every step they paled and by the time he'd run a few hundred yards they were gone. The grass beneath his feet withered and the forest he approached, the one that marked the field's end, faded to nothing before he'd even made it half way there.

He would run all night until he could run no more, exhausted and dripping with sweat. he'd drop to his knees.

And something would touch his shoulder, something would whisper into his ear.

"Pin."

And he would wake with a scream. And that was how he knew it was a dream, for on waking all fear drained from him. Replaced by the dullest edge of discomfort. Replaced by slate coloured walls and bed and flesh. Here he sometimes couldn't tell where he began and the world ended. Everything was the same.

* * *

Glass smashed.

At first Pin did not pay much attention. Then something smashed again then tinkled. A crisper, clearer sound than anything he had heard in an age. Pin tilted his head and frowned.

No, it couldn't be.

He dropped the book, which he had been reading for the fiftieth time, and ran to the storage rooms.

What he saw did not surprise him.

Sendle and his men were destroying the townsfolk's kaleidoscopes. The glass beads greyed as soon as they tumbled from their magical casing.

Pin tried to stop them, a soldier backhanded him.

"What is this?" He demanded as he picked himself up from the floor.

"Colour is addictive," Sendle said. "It is disruptive, destroying the townsfolk's morale. It will be banned."

Pin stared at him in astonishment; the king's man had grown in stature. He alone had thrived in Pin's ill-made world. Perhaps if he had spun a different spell . . .

"You can't do that. Colour is their truest link to the past."

Sendle gripped Pin's shoulders.

"This world you have made is perfection. Why should we desire the gaudy, the frail, when endlessness—or near enough—awaits us? It is time to turn away from these meaningless follies. It is time for discipline."

He stared out at the grey landscape, twisted his face into a grey smile.

"There is no need for colour, Pin. There is no need for past."

"And what does the king say of this?"

Sendle shrugged his shoulders.

"The King lies abed, staring at his own kaleidoscope. Occasionally one of his lackeys will shake it for him. He says there are whole worlds in there. The King rules another realm now."

* * *

Pin stared at the staff. It lay upon a silk pillow. Pulsing gently, releasing the minimum amount of energy required to keep their tiny universe going. His fingers brushed it, tips stinging.

When he touched it, his body ignited with sensation.

The staff was in his safekeeping. After all Pin had created it, no one but he understood its maintenance.

On an impulse he picked it up and walked to the window.

For a moment colour smudged the town. It was quiet. It was always so quiet these days. More townsfolk were found every day in their beds with rods in their skulls, blabbering fervidly of reds and yellows and blues.

Sendle had the rods removed and the culprits thrown in the dungeon. However, the devices were becoming more sophisticated, secretive: small glass rods, worn beneath hats, held in place by metal caps.

People wandered the streets silently, tapping their heads, making the world a secret kaleidoscope.

* * *

Night and the sky was grey. Or was it morning?

Pin could no longer tell. He stood atop the castle; his telescope had once sat up here. But he'd dismantled it to make one of the kaleidoscopes.

Pin gazed at the silent city below—a few figures stumbled furtively down the streets—then across at the void beyond the border. When he gripped the staff tightly, colour danced there and possibility.

"But, of course, it will mean my death. All of our deaths most probably."

He thought he heard someone whisper his name.

Pin raised the staff high then smashed it against the wall, and even as the staff shattered he felt a growing satisfaction. Fingers stinging, he dropped the broken shards of glass. The earth shuddered, once, violently. Pin fell hard on his rear and looked at the sharp and flaring scatterings of his madness. Fear and loathing and joy filled him all at once. He got to his feet and gazed around.

Everywhere flowers bloomed. The streets below and the once cold, grey ashlar became a florist's delight, as stone and wood gave birth to panicles, spikes and corymbs of petalled brilliance. Great trusses of blooms dipped heavy in reds and yellows and blues from the wizard's hair.

Pin laughed and waited. Though he did not have to wait too long.

There was a clattering of armour and hard-soled boots.

Sendle marched out onto the tower top, five guards behind him, all their clothes and weapons weighted with flowers.

"Pin, you have cursed our world with bounty. You have undone us all." Sendle's red face was a mask of shock—and what a surprise it was to see such an expression on such a rosy cheeked man.

The guards closed around the wizard. Pin stretched out his pale arms and let them be bound with black iron. The metal burnt his wrists—iron is such cruelty to wizards.

"I am sorry, Sendle. Very sorry, but it had to end." He winced, his flesh smoking but, even the smoke was colourful, a wonderful pale blue. "You must understand."

From below echoed great cheers. In the distance verdigris-fringed bells rang out. A mile west a forest sprouted, grew tangled and dewy.

Sendle shook his head, his rubbery red lips pursed, his black locks gleaming.

"Wizard, you have doomed us all."

* * *

"It is the end," King Catchincraw said. "A mighty undoing."

His grey beard kept sprouting flowers; in one hand he held

the court's kaleidoscope. He let the tube drop. It cracked open; beads skittered across the stone floor. A half-dozen courtiers rushed to pick them up. The King waved them away.

"You waste your time. Such colours are not precious." He plucked a bouquet from his beard, and hurled it at their faces. "See. See!"

He looked down and realised that his skin was fringed with grass.

The king laughed and picked at the green and tickling blades. There was not much else he could do.

* * *

A storm was coming.

The iron had softened into a wreath of wattle, supple and forgiving of the burns on his wrist. He bent his head over the chopping block, which sprouted like arms new branches, and waited.

"Let's get this over and done," King Catchincraw growled, and waved at his man-at-arms.

Sendle read out the charge—all he had left to him now was his duty. Pin knew that and would not take it from him: a voice, less than a whisper, called his name, but he did not fear it.

"For releasing bounty upon the world, for unlocking fecundity, you are sentenced to death."

The wizard met Sendle's eyes. "I was already dead—worse than dead. Smell the air, executioner, and the rain. Smell the spring. Without these we have been but corpses for years."

Sendle snarled. "Bounty will kill us, wizard." He brought the axe down hard. "As it has killed you."

Pin's head, eyes blinking, fell to the ground. Butterflies burst from the tumbling blood, shaking out blood-droplet wings and fluttering into the air. Sendle swung at them ineffectually with his dutiful axe, dropping it at last to stare up at the bruised sky.

"Bounty, damn it. Damn it all."

The butterflies flew into the storm, their lives as swiftly beating as their red velvety wings.

And the rain began to fall.

DRIFT

She e-mailed me again today. The message made it through God knows how many barriers, I sat in my chair, bent over the screen and masturbated as I devoured that tiny electronic missive and thought of S—pale flesh, the soft curve of her belly, and her dark eyes always serious, always cautious. It's funny but I can only clearly see her when I reach orgasm.

What we had was special, but like everything it has somehow all gone wrong.

    D.

How are things in down there? Have they gotten the pumps working again? Heard the power grid has been holding. Hope you are okay?

Love

S

PS Will send a longer e later. Promise:-)

I bought a gun yesterday. The kids next door did me a deal. Guns are illegal, so it was only logical that they would have them for sale. They sell all sorts of drugs too; the hard stuff the powders and the sugars. Now I've got the gun and, more importantly, they know I've got it, they might think twice before breaking in again.

They're always breaking in. Caught a pair of them screwing on my grandmother's bed—now the spare bed. They just laughed in my face. Never been so scared or angry in all my life. Kids these days.

My back has been acting up again. Had to carry the groceries all the way from the supermarket—not that my work-pension-grant can stretch to more than the bare necessities. Still a young woman from downstairs offered to blow me for an apple—her eyes were black and hungry. I felt bad after I came—with S's face in my mind's eye—I always do, gave her the whole bag. I'm luckier than a lot of people around here. Still an apple would be nice, one day the fruit might make it home.

The sky hasn't changed these last four years, looks like a big wound and we still get half a dozen or so ships passing overhead during the day, belching smoke and spray, going God alone knows where. During the evening there is an almost endless procession of them—engines burring up the stillness of the night, static constancy to blur and fuse with the gunshots. They're coloured like circus tents, bright reds and yellows and blues. Sometimes music is piped down to us, kaleidoscopes of sound—madness in that wounded sky.

One of the big ships crashed a few weeks ago. By the time I got there they'd stoned the pilot to death—dressed in a clown suit, smeared with their rage, the colours of his raiment already fading, the quality of the cloth degrading on contact with our air, he looked like a broken toy—a kid was pissing on his powdered face, pissing and laughing. The few soldiers that had been called could do nothing. Outnumbered and weary they just stood around and shrugged their shoulders. Some of them even helped with the looting of the airship's ruined gondola—pulling free crates of alien machinery, odd clumps of wire and cogs, nothing at all compatible with our technologies. This is another world's bounty. The ships are just passing through, like everything else —they're not meant to be here, but somehow they are.

I pulled out my notepad—the one that used to inspire so much fear—and a young child snatched it out of my hands. I know where he lives and I have my gun. I could turn those chuckles carmine with one thunderous retort.

I memorised the names using a technique I learnt at university.

Dear D,

you never write. Do you even get these `e's? Winter's such a depressing time. They're shutting down the factories here. The men are getting angry, some are very violent. None of us ever wanted this. You never wanted this, did you? The King is dead. Did you hear about that? Suicide, slit his own throat with a penknife. The newspapers keep talking about it as a metaphor. The Prime Minister has come out of it all looking very strong and assured the words he said in the public broadcast were just the sort of thing to win votes.

Did we ever marry D? Did I ever kiss you that night in the clouds with the city in bright tatters beneath us?

Love, s

Yes.

Last evening was a nightmare. Something got up on the roof and ran and stumbled and ran. Backwards and forwards. Clumping and clanging and shrieking like a demon. First I thought it was a dream. My Uncle spoke to me, voice that hideous screaming, and I knew my parents were dead again and again.

I woke with my gun cold and hard against my skin, their old death in the room, chill and disorienting, and the shrieking running creature on the tin roof above. After a few more minutes of that someone shot it. Quiet settled in quickly, someone next door cheered.

I got up—heart pounding—and tried to access the Internet.

The signal was too bad, something about Jupiter I later read in the paper. Still at about five o'clock I managed to get her e-mail. I will find her one day. I will remind her. She is so wrong, I have replied to everything she has ever sent. They just never get through. That she keeps sending me messages must mean something.

Went into the city today. The track's only good till halfway between Milton and Roma St stations. Everyone piled off there and we walked into town, picking our way through the thistles and over algae-choked puddles in the train tracks, the catenaries hanging above us coated with moss and the webs of spiders larger than my hand—I've seen them catch birds, watched them bind shrieking herons in funereal silk, the spiders are plump, the birds cautious and the trains still. Public transport is now public procession; we march into a city that is dead.

The Captain was in. He greeted me as he always does, warmly but distantly. Says I am helping with the effort. Today it wasn't enough and I asked him if it really matters. If any of it really matters any more. For a moment that warmth fled, I swear something nearly snapped in him, and his voice grew chill and almost menacing.

Things will work out. Solutions will be found. The world's gone wrong but it can be righted. Everybody Must Play Their Part.

But it's getting worse. Half of George Street isn't there any more. Queen St Mall is a ruin, a winding bad land in the heart of the city, habitation of madmen, of howls and thunderous applause—but then we've all gone mad these days.

I have other friends in the city. Members of various public sectors who remember that it wasn't always like this.

They tell me that it's all going to hell here.

On the way back the train breaks down—shudders to stillness just outside Taringa. We pass the driver, he is on the intercom and weeping, and I know that this is the last time I'm ever likely to catch that train. Someone mumbles something about cutbacks.

I'm five hours in getting back home. Used to take me twenty minutes.

Dear D,

sometimes I wish I'd never left you. That we'd both gone to England together. I don't think they'll ever get the commercial planes running again. Eighty Crashes in one day. I'll never really understand it. When the damn Yanks or Russians or the Chinese undid reality, they really fucked us all. God, I miss your kisses. I don't think you'd like it here. Rains all the time. I hated the heat in Brisbane but sometimes I yearn for it—the blood heat of the air.

Do you still go to that place where we drank coffee? Do you still smoke those blasted cheap cigarettes?

Love,

S

The place where we drank coffee is gone. A cold wind blows through its ruin, and some dark and mumbling presence, perhaps a memory that is only half a memory. On occasion I find myself standing there, peering in at the shadow-haunted wreckage. I see the coffee machines at the back, they've fallen, spilled upon the ground, something glimmers there, spins and winks. I always leave feeling that my gaze has been returned. By what though I do not know.

No one smokes these days. It's bad for you.

There is death in the air. I walk with a scarf wrapped around my face, and still I breathe it in. The gun sits in my pocket.

The fridge packed it in last night.

They're making love in my bed when I get home. I shoot them until they stop moving.

I bury the bodies outside—just kids. The neighbours won't

bother me for a while. The soil is fecund and loamy it smells like my childhood, I remember digging for worms. Perhaps I'll plant some tomatoes here. I dig and think of S and how even the finest things can go bad, how every dream I've ever had has twisted, grown distorted and mocking about me.

A ship drifts above, all carnival colours; I am drenched in its leavings, the sky stained with smoke and spume. I lift the gun up and put it to my head.

Dear D

there is always hope isn't there? Wasn't that the last thing in Pandora's box? Nothing can kill that. We'll meet again I'm sure.

Love always,

S

PS

Last night I dreamt you were dead and riding a great balloon—like the ghost of Dumont. You were laughing. Don't think I have ever seen you so happy. Will write a longer e next time. Promise.

TO END ALL

I am and be the straight jacket of me flesh and me thought, which is part of the territory of living. And this is the war to end all wars at the edge of the Temporal Abyss.

You ever come down, with the pool of gravity awash, all vengeance, with right on your side and the viciousness of your shells? I've rained Hell on me enemies, rained the blasts of Hell and the undoing of radioactives.

This world we tore up is like Future, Past and Present—but the dictionaries and meanings in me brain get wiped first wave out—'cause the enemies got some big as sun pulse packager and me whole platoon's got stunned and our 'lectrics are done for—so I don't know the science of it. But the pricks got theirs in their faces 'cause the pulse came back, all echoed and twice wild, and took out their front.

We still got AIs and shit way back, 'cause the word's still coming down and we've dug in and the big guns are firing. Lighting up the skies like the second coming, with angels turned to thunderbolts and iron.

Onomatopoeia is RINGING in me rapped up skull, but I can still shoot the bastards 'cross the dead man's land, which used to be pasture but now's all churned to shit and blood and the upreaching hands of friends or foes.

It's hard to tell who's who. In wars everyone's the same, just weeping meat and stinking fear.

Me mate, Charlie Gun with his photos of his girl reckons he believes it's all a big mistake; that we're fighting ourselves, that HQ made a mess Temporal-Spatial-wise.

I say,

"You full of shit, Charlie."

Charlie smiles,

"I full of blood and dead man's land is hungry for it."

He's mighty prophetic, 'cause he takes a bullet in the throat like the very next day.

I remember certain chivalries and sophisticated ways, but that was when all me brain wasn't the baked thing it is now. I can't get much sense, but the past was pretty and there's a girl there—her kisses sweet—and a country and it's what we're fighting for. So's they tells us from up the line.

Now all I taste is ashes and dust.

We's over the top, few days later; a charge and a blasting. I finds meself struggling with some mad bastard, and he fucking guts me, but I gut him back and we're both falling, tangled like lovers, with blood and bowel everywhere and I look into the face of me killer and it's mine.

His eyes widen and mine likewise. He struggles to speak, but all I can hear is laboured breaths and the most meaningful expression is the blood that spills from broken lips, like the blood in me mouth.

Then the big guns boom, and me eye's on the sky, obliterated with colours like Death's garden all blooming in some dark springtime.

I holds me own hand and squeeze and then the shells start falling.

NAKED

i

On the seventh hour after the Godling victory—all our dreamings come to naught—Cerdic and I plunged into the fire of a black hole's rim, where photons give hollow screams and bend themselves still. The universe gone mad surrounded us and we trusted our souls to the technology of the Majestic.

"She's all burn and brimstone, Beatrice." Cerdic roared, as our suits' quantum machinery played wild anger with the nature of reality.

"The Godlings have won."

"Not yet!' Cerdic laughed, and brushed my unmade face. "Not Yet!"

The universe rushed and twisted about us. Our suits' readings were best ignored, and then.

And then nothing.

We stared into darkness absolute, and in that void our past flared up; magnificent and doomed.

ii

Cerdic kissed my brow as I unlaced his skin. Speaking in genotype, the colloquy of DNA. I felt his warming love and, dimly, the outer chill, the vacuum that fell away from the membrane of our Shell.

We hung, a single drop of amber, in a darkness perfect but for the distant smudge of stars.

"Beatrice, my Beatrice."

He held my face in lengthening fingers and I stroked the wave-form of his love, felt and caressed each new-made possibility that branched and burst from him.

The Universe went out.

Cerdic's face tightened. I glanced at him, eye's milk white and feeding as my epidermis grazed on the bubble and squeak of real and unreal particles.

"What was that?"

His brow crinkled, he gripped his chin in thought, that most ancient of gestures.

"A myriad of Ways collapsed. I do believe that—"
Nothing.

"—something is making a mess of reality.' Cerdic glanced at the dials and crystalline structures that made up the control panel of the *Mantis*. 'Things are warping at greater and greater—"

"Godlings," we whispered in unison. "The Silver Calm has come." We readied the ship. Contingencies had been made.

Possibilities vanished—sealed up behind us—as the *Mantis* ran the Thread, the space that veins and surrounds the Ways. She burst with half a million of her sisters upon the Core Plane, where the Majestic were already waiting.

iii

"We do not have much time." The Majestic whispered.

"We do not."

"The Silver Calm has come. The Machinery of Ages."

Cerdic smiled and whispered in my ear, what I already knew. He liked to appear wise.

"'They've never liked our chaos. Our manipulation of the interstices that make up the universe."

Around us four spheres spun and unwarped this sector of reality. We phased in an out and made bitter talk of war.

The Silver Calm, a collective of once metal dreams as taut as wire. Our children had turned. Poor brute machines, they sought order and saw us for what we were—the chaos from which they had come.

Old flesh and its makings were no longer to be tolerated.

iv

"Unmaker's," Cerdic cried in that depthless darkness, and, through magics I could not dream of, I heard his wild voice. "Buggerer's of reality. Well, one more card there is to play.'"

Cerdic, dreamer, lover, child. We had fused a half dozen times and gone our separate ways. I'd tasted his kisses beneath the light of a billion different stars. We had warped space and time with laughter on our lips. The suits linked us now. I felt his heartbeat, his grey thought. Though not the hidden truth. Even the deep magic of this gravity denial could not give me that.

I followed him for reasons I could not fathom. I followed him because I loved.

I wished for truth and found only reverie.

v

Of the Majestic there were only ever a handful. A race of makers and theorists, they created our finest instruments and designed the suits that Cerdic and I wore. The Majestic had lost their own universe to their own version of the Silver Calm. It had been all their kind could do to escape. Few had managed that.

Majestic Nin wept as he fused our flesh to these greatest of technical marvels and I wept with him.

Enhancement was the only way. Our natural defences were not enough against the raw computing power of the Silver Calm.

I could warp and sink into the curvature of realities. I could unpick and measure possibilities. We all had these skills, but not in the abundance of the machines.

How much like the enemy must we become to win this war?

The *Campbell* and *Gold* were our flagships, the greatest of the two tiered fleet. They led the assault on the seething forms of the Silver Calm collectives. Hammering home our reality, slamming against the onrush of their waveforms.

We the last remnants of flesh engaging our children, demanding our reality.

They were too many. Godlings swarmed about our ships and made strange measurements and curious and deadly hypotheses and undid our fleet with their readings. Reality whispered and universes collided.

The *Gold* dissipated in a cloud of hydrogen, quickly gobbled by the Zeus and Omam collectives—most ancient branch of the Silver Calm. The *Campbell* turned inside out and became streamers of itself.

Our fleet was undone in ways disparate and ironic. I watched one ship change to a block of Edwardian buildings. Moustached men on Penny-Farthings exploded in space. Ships twisted and devoured their own, became sacks of spiders. Even the Majestic succumbed, or their golden ship did, perhaps, at the last, they fled this universe as they fled their own.

The war, as all wars do and this more than any other, became madness. Chaos.

Cerdic grabbed my hand and fled through folds in the firmament.

vi

Cerdic was always closed to me. But flashing eyes and biting teeth and long and knowing fingers gave me so much.

I sensed his gaze.

"Not far to go, my love!"

I smiled hesitantly.

"How long have we been falling."

"Forever!" Cerdic laughed. "We have been falling forever."

So true. Though our suits warped time, and subjectively, but minutes passed. Like ants we crawled on the edge of a ocean as vast as the universe.

Cerdic saw it first and, in his plunge, he jabbed a finger down—or was it up—and our linked eyes observed the unobservable.

"Singularity." He breathed.

We stared into the seethe of the singularity: our suits bathed in the substance of stars, a universe of light. I still could not shake the madness of this thing and its possibilities. Here all rules were broken and all defeats could be made into victories.

We waltzed like silver fireflies in the belly of that black hole, no simulacra, but flesh ghosting in waves of intense gravity. Shrunk to the density of a quark, our mass was that of suns.

The suits, with their quantum machinery, projected their own twistings of reality. A trillion, trillion calculations and tweakings of my mind; to make of this vision something meaningful; to slow and speed things up so that I might defy gravity's tricks. Though I existed in swift flickerings of virtual particles—each atom manipulated individually then linked as a one—I felt as of meat and bone and the suit made me whole.

Cerdic touched me, held me, kissed me and I felt all these things. His fingers brushed at the mad tangle of my hair.

"Well, my love, we've made this night time dance. Partnered ourselves to its end."

Lips touched mine again and then he fell away into—

I heard his fevered breathing, as he bound himself in its fractured chaos and turned towards me, his face a fiery stare. He fused himself to ice and flame and a glorious infinity.

'Tis but round one!' He roared and, momentarily, I mourned that, in his rapturous fury, he did not say goodbye.

His suit flared out in a burst of virtual protons and, with it, the rage of a singularity made naked. A freeing of the impossible. The universe ended for the singularity is an end and a beginning. I rode a wave of particles unleashed and for an eon or two lost my mind.

vii

I drift. My suit encloses me and slows and speeds things up as necessary. Light has changed its speed twice since Cerdic unbound the singularity and made anew the universe. Things are shifting down to some kind of stasis.

We have won.

I eject, at seven second intervals, strands of matter. Genotyping information, the map and memory of our universe. Behind me the stars flower and I hear your thoughts as a liminal laughing buzz.

My suit contains you all and you, Cerdic, sweet child, it holds you as well. The Majestic promised that.

I drift, a naked seedling. I drift and wait for what I've sown to find me.

Dear Cerdic, I wait for you.

TAR BABY

"This is too dangerous. You must go back."

I teetered on the edge of the world, contemplating the fall, as lightning bursts revealed the rocks far below: the gnawed-on bones of the Earth against which the TAR lapped. Here hunger slept. Here, to far beyond the horizon, the TAR slept.

A storm drew near, its boiling rage odd against the placid surface beneath it. Yet the TAR was its source.

"Harmony," George said. "Harmony this is not safe. There is no way I can transmit a signal from here."

I grinned in the face of that storm, a dry, electric wind already beginning to tangle my hair.

"Not safe! Not safe! Not safe!" The ozone-bitter wind tore the words from my mouth.

The compound a kilometre to the East was safe. My mother and my father always ensured that I was safe. George lectured me often on the various protocols of safety, had lectured me on this very trip, all along the path from home, through the dusty coil of road trailing between the eucalypts and then up into the stony hills against which the TAR found softly shivering pause.

Here, and only here, was I not monitored, coddled, made safe. At this edge of the world all I had to put up with was

George. Eight years of living with an AI in your skull can make you very adept at ignoring them.

Here I was free.

The moon was a ruined white eye glaring down and I stared up at it, then followed its wan gaze to the quietly stirring darkness.

The Lunar Militia created the TAR.

Tautomerically Aggressive Replicators. They called it the Last Resort and with it the LM very nearly won their war of independence. Nearly.

A single pellet grew to swallow North America, another buried China. Central Australia was gone, an inland sea of pure, mechanised night. Earth Security barely managed to stop its flow, and send the TAR to sleep. By then the planet was decimated, weather systems shattered, ecosystems turned to sludge. Wild storms still raged across the TAR, though they were decreasing in frequency.

Above, the moon had several new craters, black scars of a war that reshaped two worlds.

I shivered and stared west and all was storm or the thick, placid sheen of the TAR. This was once wheat-belt country. A wild and fertile land, occasionally drowned by floods, eucalypts dotting the transient oceans of brown water. Now it hadn't rained for almost a century and I had never seen a flood beyond the simulations in the virtual constructs of the compound's playpens.

Though storms played constantly over the surface of the TAR they were vast, electric and dry.

"Harmony."

"Not safe," I mocked and jumped up and down on this edge of the world.

But the storm was increasing in intensity and the darkness below, that had once been trees and soil and people, suddenly made me feel cold. And I imagined the TAR, and all the souls consumed by it, staring up asking why I mocked.

Time to leave, I thought and turned, but then the earth beneath me crumbled. Gasping, I slipped and the world toppled.

"HARMONY!"

Everything slowed down and I felt George slide into the driver's seat of my body and I knew it was serious. I was oddly calm(safe)as he threw me into a spin. My fingers snapped out and brushed, for a moment, the ledge.

But it was too late and too much had fallen with me.

I felt the burn of his irritation at missing our grip as he pulled me into a foetal curl and generated the crash cocoon. I tried to move my eyes and for a moment, before it was all gone, I could see the rocks and I was plummeting towards them.

I called out for my mother. Then there was dark.

* * *

This is a dream

In the dark that was not dark—for things moved with a kind of fractured intensity, absolute clarity shifting to shadows—I bobbed and spun and my mother kissed my face.

Just a single peck on the cheek, but it was warm and comforting.

I did not fear the dark, but then I had always had George and he had always made me feel safe.

This is a dream

There was a single burst of lightning. A sheet of fire that crossed the heavens of this restless darkness.

A ghost whispered in my ear and then.

This is the truth within the dream.

Three beeps, piercing and short. Three beeps again, then a soft and constant beating that I knew was in time with my heart.

"Harmony, you should be awake now."

"I can't see."

George's calming presence surrounded me.

"I know, but you are safe."

"Where am I?"

"Safe, you are safe."

"George, where am I?"

"Eight Kilometers from the Western Edge and riding the current away from the shore at approximately seventeen metres a minute."

"I can't move." I realised that I was subvocalising. I tried to speak naturally, but couldn't move my mouth. The chirruping of my heart turned to a racing.

"Calm down, Harmony. Calm down, my child. You are quite safe, I am here. All systems are functional." My mind's eye flickered then flared to life. The darkness transformed into a series of readings, at first insubstantial, I let my mind envelope them until they became a constant stream of numbers, soothing but meaningless.

George seemed to sense this and the readings transformed into a cartoon representation of a crash cocoon—a funny looking cotton ball floating in darkness.

"You are here." A tiny me appeared inside the cocoon, that tiny me grinned, then waved. I wished that I could wave back, or even smile and I thought that I was much prettier than the cartoon me. George sighed. "Please, allow me a little poetic licence."

"Okay," I said.

Around the crash cocoon, the TAR flowed, its movements represented by a swirl of arrows. The image pulled back, giving a sense of depth, revealing the distance of the cocoon from the surface. I noticed that the cocoon was not only drifting from the shore but sinking.

"We are surrounded by semi-active materials. Harmony, we are in the TAR and you are safe."

I shivered. My nose was itchy and I wanted to scratch it, but couldn't move. The cocoon enclosed me completely, if I tried really hard I could feel its fibres against my tongue. For a moment I was gripped with a desire to thrash and tear against my prison. But I couldn't move, no matter how hard I wanted to, to do so would kill me.

"So what can we do?" I asked George. And for the first time in my life I listened intently to his reply.

* * *

"Here you are in a highly suggestible state," George said and I felt a warmth from him that may have been a smile. "So let me suggest something a little more comfortable."

I sat in a classroom, alone but for the teacher, who scribbled furiously on the blackboard. I could smell the chalk, there was a window to my right through which sunlight slanted. George stopped his scribbling and turned towards me.

I had to laugh.

"That's some moustache you've got there."

George smiled and twirled its tips.

"You think so?"

"No."

George shrugged his narrow shoulders.

"Well I like it." He cleared his throat. "Now on to the subject at hand."

George motioned towards the board.

The TAR was dragging me away from the Western Edge and there was nothing I could do about it. The chalk realigned itself into a set of diagrams, marking the position of the cocoon and its relation to the receding shore.

"There will be some kind of search. That much is certain. However, our monitor and telemetric systems cannot get through. There is just too much static generated by the TAR."

George frowned.

"Resources are limited. Keeping you alive is of the utmost import and there is not a lot of oxygen in the TAR. I have slowed your body down into a kind of metahybernation, but I can only take it so far. The more I slow you down, the slower I run.

"I am also preparing to extend an aerial, but it will take some time. TAR is suggestible to a degree and has much potential as a building material, but I would hardly call it highly malleable."

"How long?" I asked.

"Quite some time."

I had never known George to be so evasive.

"Please tell me."

George's eyes softened.

"Nearly a year. You see, I have to stabilise us first. This involves the restructuring of the cocoon. That alone will take a couple of months."

Somewhere deep inside me I felt a scream rising. I could not move nor see and twelve months separated me from any chance of freedom. Still, that terror lay deep below.

"I'm keeping it there," George said. "Fear is highly aerobic. It would be bad. It might harm you."

I shivered and knew that the AI could only shield me so far. That I was safe, but only for now.

"Can't you just put me to sleep?"

"To put you to sleep might kill you. I cannot risk that, Harmony. I am not programmed that way." He sat down in the seat before mine and said quietly. "I am dependent on your neurological processes for my own functioning. You are as close to asleep as I can allow, suspended in dreams. Harmony, I have created as optimal a kind of homeostasis as possible. Your nutrient is being provided intravenously through the assimilation of a kind of anaerobic bacteria that has somehow found a niche in the TAR—sure example of the tenacity of life, even here. If you were to sleep it would shut me down as well, so instead everything has been slowed down, except your brain.

"So how am I going to pass the time?"

I felt George's amusement.

"Learn."

And that is what I did.

* * *

Drifting on an ocean of dreaming, I studied all that George could teach me. However, he was not an educational unit. George's database was odd and fragmentary, stuff that the programmers had downloaded in an apparently arbitrary manner. George was meant as a companion and guardian, yes. A trustworthy and compassionate friend. But his main purpose was as a security system, a safeguard. So many children were lost in the war.

In a few months time an educational unit would have been downloaded to compliment George. As a guardian George proved more than adequate, as a teacher he did the best he could.

I learnt the CNO cycle of stars, but not about their positions in the heavens. I memorised Woodrow Wilson's *Covenant of the League of Nations* but did not know how they failed. I could recite all of Blake's Songs of Innocence, but knew nothing of bitter experience or that these poems were separated from me by over five hundred years.

Sometimes I walked the gardens of Versailles or across a Sydney Harbour Bridge prior to the LM's Rapier S&D strike of 72. A girl drifting on imaginary legs, alone but for the voice of her AI.

Indeed, over that time I lost the sense of having legs at all, or real hands or arms. I was just a consciousness in a vivid world created through the AI's circuitry and sensory deprivation. But my mouth always felt parched and dry and sometimes my eyes itched, and I could neither drink nor scratch.

One day George paused in the middle of a lesson—the first probe had touched down on Europa and started drilling—and smiled. He twirled one moustache tip and bowed ever so slightly.

"We have stabilised," he said. "I can start generating the aerial."

"How long until it reaches the surface," I asked.

"A while," George said.

I left it at that.

* * *

Something jarred the cocoon and my vision hazed and the gardens around me shivered. For a moment I was gripped with vertigo.

"Your inner ear," George explained. "I know it is difficult, but just try to ignore it."

George created an image of the external world, and in the murk of the TAR I could just make out a shape swimming slowly away.

"What was that?"

"I believe that we have encountered something entirely new. Part of the TAR has become analoguous to life."

More of the shapes began to gather around the cocoon. For the first time in a long while I felt crowded in. I shivered and a chill swept up my spine.

"Can they hurt us?"

"I do not think so." George paused. "Harmony this is remarkable. The TAR has somehow found a way to merge with the bacteria. Every one of those creatures is packed with them.

Evolutionary processes are playing out at an incredible rate. It appears that not all of the TAR is made up of semi active nano-machines."

"Some of it looks very active to me."

One fish-like TAR creature swallowed another.

"As long as they don't eat me I'm happy." I looked at the Aerial playing out behind me. "And as long as they don't eat that."

"I think I should work on thickening the aerial up."

* * *

This new external world gripped me. And I found more and more of my time spent observing it. I had grown tired of my ghost-like existence wandering half-explained corridors of the world. Here was something that was actually happening.

The world of the TAR was in constant flux. Great behemoths would swallow smaller creatures only to be eaten inside out, breaking into tiny clusters that were again consumed.

"It is information," George explained. "Bacteria often do it. They aren't so much hunting, but trading. Evolutionary progressions are spread throughout the TAR by consumption."

At these depths things had begun to change. Here the TAR generated its own light. Much of it was translucent rather than opaque and according to what George could reveal, tinged with colours as varied and splendid as reef coral. Only the creatures themselves exhibited little colouring, remaining as dark as the TAR on the surface. In these vivid depths the creatures stood out. Smooth dark shadows swimming in a rainbow.

If they possessed intelligence it was hard to tell. However, I noticed one thing about them. They seemed to find me as fascinating as I found them.

* * *

The aerial rose slowly and not an hour went by that I didn't think about it or where it was going and who lived beyond the surface of my prison. Were they still looking?

I couldn't imagine my parents ever giving up. I imagined their grief and wondered if it matched my own. Of course, it would and more so, for I knew that I was alive. They had nothing but the TAR.

There was an analogue of that too in George's catalogue of virtual worlds. A replica of my edge of the World. Sometimes I would stand there, staring down. On occasion I'd step off, George never let me fall. I was doing enough of that already.

Slowly, slowly, painfully slowly, a millimetre at a time. The aerial rose. And slowly I began to lose interest in the world.

Increasingly, I found myself drawn to that one virtual world. Looking into the depths, that black mass revealed nothing. I would not move, not a virtual muscle, just stare and, far away, on the horizon a storm boiled but it did not draw near. Like me it was frozen in time.

* * *

One day, as I stood on the virtual edge of the world, George spoke to me. Not as a teacher or a guardian, but as a friend.

"Harmony, I have failed." His eyes were sad. "I have done everything to keep you going, to feed your body. But there just aren't enough resources here. So I did what I could. Over the last few months I have had to restructure you physically."

His hand brushed my head.

"Harmony, there is nothing left of your body as you know it but a brain, fed by long filaments of lungs. But even that is not enough. There is too little oxygen down here."

He squeezed my hand.

"Harmony, I have failed you. But I will not let you die."

In my world of dreams I turned to him.

"But what choice do you have?"

And then he told me.

The TAR was nothing but machinery. Nothing but replicating muck gone wild. But it could be modified.

"I have been modifying it for months. I believe I can modify it again, at least so far as to create a kind of network complex enough to upload our minds." George looked at me almost excitedly. "The TAR has just been waiting for something to tell it what to do. What to be."

"And what would it mean for me?" I asked.

George took his time in answering.

"I don't really know. But it is the only alternative I can offer you."

I sighed.

"George, I want to go home. I don't want to stay here forever."

George held my hand.

"Maybe we can fix that too. Maybe part of you can go home. But Harmony, I don't think all of you can go. Once we do what we are about to, you will always be part of the TAR. But so will I. This will fuse us, more closely than you can know." He smiled. "I will never leave you. Now what do you want? This is your choice, Harmony. I cannot make it for you."

I tightened my grip on his hand.

"Let's go."

Together we stepped over the edge.

* * *

Exponetial expansion. I felt myself falling. George was letting me fall. Not safe. Not safe at all. I was a storm where all the raindrops could comprehend the exact spatial position and thoughts of the others.

Am I me? Or a wave.

"Neither," something that could have been George replied.

And then I was.

When do we stop.

We do not know.

The creatures of the TAR were on the verge of sentience.

We are on the verge of thought.

She spread her consciousness and we raced out. Consuming, being consumed, changing. Each one her eyes. Each one her voice; a single glorious cry. She reached the surface of the TAR. Extended a hundred gleaming tentacles and breathed the airwaves into her. In a second her network had downloaded the entire communications web and then she paused.

She had found a picture of her mother. We had found a picture of our father. We wept.

Reports detailing a girl lost. A search that proved fruitless. And then nothing. Just a few messages her mother had sent to friends.

I miss her.

We move too fast. We will be detected. We cannot unmake what we have begun, but . . .

Plans are made.

* * *

Once unlocked, the TAR is so mutable. It does not consume but can create. Me and then it. A crash cocoon rises to the surface. Signals are sent out and soon a vehicle flies over then another.

The cocoon is lifted away and the TAR watches it go.

Part of it is softly, sadly jealous of that which it shall never have. Mother. Father. But it is its own family.

Then its thoughts, our thoughts, turn elsewhere and its growth continues. Its tidal sentience. So much potential, one part of that mind looks to the stars.

In time. In time.

* * *

Here is where you fell, George says.

Sometimes you just have to go back, even if it takes years.

I stand on an edge of the world and stare down. A storm is coming, they come less frequently now. The TAR does not generate as much electricity as it once did. It stores it deeper, like some sort of secret. The TAR divulges little.

When I was younger, they pulled me from it. My crash cocoon barely functioning after nearly a year adrift, everyone amazed that I could have survived such an ordeal. TAR Baby they called me.

I am not amazed at all for I had George. And all I can remember of that time is falling. Just falling and never hitting bottom.

The TAR took so much away, but just this once it gave something back.

Why did the TAR release me? How did I survive?

Sometimes I dream that I am on a sea of night, then I am sinking. Finally, I am the sea, an endlessness of consciousness. Incomprehensible and alert.

Sometimes I don't think the TAR ever let me go. That I am still in its grasp and that I grasp back. But I've told you these things, holding your hand as I hold it now.

I stand on an edge of the world.

Be careful, George murmurs and I take a step back and you pull me into your arms.

Still, I am staring down at the dark. And I can't shake the feeling that it is staring back.

CAROUSEL

She is going to die.

I struggled from a dream of emptiness to that, first horrible waking thought, and reached to touch her, but my hand stopped before it completed the movement. Everything was uncertain, because everything was certain. Evelyn lay stretched next to me, skin warm, her breathing deep and constant. I set my heart to those breaths.

It seemed more dream than reality, a cruel and empty dream to be discarded by the opening of morning eyes. But it was not, I had woken from dreams to this. I reached for my notebook and whispered it on.

"She is going to die." I watched the words flow across the LCD. The cursor blinked on the edge of that truth. She is going to die.

"Off now."

The machine's face went out and I stared into my own.

She is going to die, my eyes said, and I put the notebook down, quietly so as not to wake her.

* * *

It was in all the Newspages.

I was oblivious to this new-sprung history. And would have

remained so except Evelyn pointed it out to me; was animated about something other than the terrible truth that hung over us.

She was fading then, and in her slow dying and my grief I'd become myopic, the outside world indistinct, ethereal. I did not seek to escape it, just could not see for the awful presence of her and the void her leaving would make.

In those last days, I had a recurring dream, horrible in its simplicity. I lived in our house alone, with no memory of her.

I wandered too large rooms, and hallways too long, tossed and turned in a bed far too big. Not sure what was missing, just that, without it, life seemed as empty as the spaces between the stars, as empty as this listless dream-bound house.

I'd wake with her beside me, sleeping, her eyes swift beneath the lids, cataloguing what dreams I did not know. Though I wished them more generous than mine. Her presence was a bitter comfort and an endless question drawing to a close. How many more nights did we have? I'd touch her, briefly, lightly, frightened even such a caress might stir her; wishing it would. And when it didn't, I'd tumble again into my terrible, empty dreams.

She woke me once, from such a nightmare, her fingers hot and persistent. For a moment I did not recognise her.

"A carousel, Stephen. They've found a carousel." She laughed at my incomprehension, and waved the computer notepad in front of me.

Three AM.

Delicately carved horses bobbed up and down, around and around. I stared with blinking, stupid eyes at a brief video downland set on cycle. The horses never made a complete circuit.

The memory is vivid, Evelyn's almost translucent skin, taut against her bones, her eyes shining as brightly as the small lamp that burned on her bedside table. I remember it not for the greater history of the moment, but for her excitement, this sudden animation. "An alien artefact. No two, maybe more. Nobody's sure. Not big, but small, very, very small."

"What? What?"

"It's been confirmed. It's everywhere. CNN. NEWSNET. BBC."

"April the first?"

"It's July."

The carousel spun, so alien and familiar. I laughed and touched her face and kissed her lips, and gazed at the wonder in her brilliant, beautiful eyes.

Doctors had discovered the first one in a tissue sample in a New York hospital; a carousel careening amongst cancer cells. Pedologists in a research station at the New South Wales town of Armidale found the second. And then they were everywhere.

Images of the carousels were posted on the web a few hours later. First the Fortean Network, then the more conventional services. These were no crop circles, elusive, inconsistent; they were everywhere and in everything.

In the flickering, and spinning and chattering of newsgroups, all I wished for was her gaze and the pleasure of her happiness and that it might never end.

Evelyn shuddered wearily. "You better get some rest, darling."

"Yes, but—" She was asleep before her head touched the pillow. I tucked the sheets around her. They seemed somehow more substantial than her flesh as though they knew she was soon to die, that they wrapped up little more than a ghost.

I stroked her face just once and made myself ready to stand sentinel over her dreams. I could not face my own.

* * *

Evelyn was weaker the next day. Too much excitement, not enough sleep. We lay in bed together for much of the morning.

"Tell me about them." She said. "I need to know."

"There's not much to know. They're calling them SDOs. Small Dumb Objects, it's a play on the old Science Fiction term Big Dumb Objects—monolithic and enigmatic alien constructions. These though are tiny and they're telling us nothing."

She frowned.

"Then make it up, you're the writer."

Writer! I hadn't managed a single paragraph since Evelyn had gotten sick. Eight months and not a single word. Evelyn was my muse. I'd made love to her with words and with her dying the well dried up. I did not want to create. I wanted only her.

"Give me a while."

Evelyn laughed.

"I don't have a while. Tell me now."

 . Here, from memory, is that tale.

Once upon a time and long ago, a race came to knowledge then science and then . . . They lived in a fairground. A wonderland. They explored their solar system, sent probes out much farther and realised that was as far as they could go and still remain what they were. Distance was a calamity to their existence.

They mined their nearby gas giants, colonised and webbed their solar system. They could manipulate space, they could shape their world exactly as they wanted it, but that was all.

Faster than light travel was possible but in the most limited of ways.

Some of them grew lonely, wanted to reach out. The universe is big; there must be something else.

They created tiny probes. Machines that rode the distances in seconds; crossing the galaxy in big bursts of light. Diving through the fabric of the universe, emerging by distant stars, relaying information.

They've covered the galaxy, maybe two. They've reached out to every sentient creature they have encountered. Perhaps they no longer live, perhaps in all that time they have stumbled into extinction or grown bored and decadent, and forgotten all that they strived for. That their legacy continued is certain. They've filled the void between the stars with their presence and now they have found us.

Evelyn was asleep by the time I had finished. I don't think I ever got the chance to explain why.

* * *

I drove Evelyn home from that place—so nurse and doctor crowded. They were all very positive. It was a friendly hospital. On more than one occasion acquaintances remarked how very lucky we were to have such a good health system in this country and to live so close to the very best.

Yes, I am lucky. My wife was dying. Lucky to have the best doctors tell me they can't really do anything, but maybe this will work . . . Sorry.

* * *

Doctor Elliott smiled somewhat sheepishly.

"We've found a carousel in your bloods. Would you like to have a look?"

Evelyn laughed.

"Of course."

The carousel spun before us delicate amongst the failing machinery of her blood, the granulocytes and corpuscles.

I held Evelyn's hand, her grip both strong and fragile. I felt the bones beneath it and the tremors that wracked her body, precursors of death.

"There's close to a million in each of us." Dr Elliott said. "They're too tiny to do any damage."

"It's beautiful." Evelyn kissed me.

* * *

In my dreams I walked an empty house, alone but for my confusion. My lover's kisses burned on my lips and I did not know what they were. My footsteps echoed and I ran, faster and faster through room after room. Running in circles and finding nothing, not even certain as to the object of my search.

All night I ran. And she was not there.

* * *

"They're suggesting that the carousels might be openings," Evelyn said, looking up from her notepad.

"Openings to what?" I said, pausing from writing another request of leave. Work had been sympathetic, but I knew I was beginning to stretch things too far.

"You'll love this. Wormholes, leading, well no one knows where they lead. Just that, over nanosecond intervals, the carousels have much more mass than they should, then much less. It could account for their spinning. Sounds a bit like your story."

She looked so very thin. Some days all I wanted to do was hold her tight, as though somehow, I might anchor her to this world. But how could I shield her, or hold her here, when the disease burned and consumed, caved in her flesh?

Sometimes I talked about her going and she would touch my lips to silence them and wipe away my tears.

"I'm not gone yet."

Sometimes I got so mad I would storm and yell and end up weeping at her lap. I always felt ashamed. Evelyn was brave for both of us, and that wasn't right.

I think I mumbled something about that at the funeral.

* * *

It was not long after Evelyn died that the Neptune probe, Demeter II, noticed the carousel at a Lagrangian point between Neptune and Triton. Twenty miles wide, spinning around and around in slow orbit of that vast blue world. From SDO to BDO. Any suggestion of a hoax faded. More probes were planned. The carousel seemed to be generating its own light. Nearby starlight appeared to red shift then blue at its passing.

I remember staring at that gigantic fairground ride and thinking of Evelyn. The lamp that burned, the fire in her eyes.

* * *

That night I dreamt of the fairground. The constant murmuring of crowd; the occasional cough; the cackles of an easily amused man; the cries of carnies and the rumble of machinery; and, above it all, the piped and frantic music of the carousel—half mad, half joyous, transcendence in the round and up and down. The fairground was empty, yet so crowded with the sounds and smells of every sideshow I have ever known. Every circus, every town show. Dung and straw and sugar. Meat sizzling.

Alone and then.

In a flickering at the corner of an eye. A fleeting movement, but one so familiar.

That night I dreamt of the fairground and it went on for forever. And she was there.

* * *

I cleaned the house properly for the first time. I lay to rest our past, as much as I could. We shared this place, of her it contained almost everything. Letting go was harder than I could have imagined. The house had become so much like those dreams. I am alone.

The night before, the distant carousel, had flared out brilliantly. So brightly that it was possible to see it, as a pinpoint of light, with the naked eye. The flash had only lasted a second then died. All the net babbled this as I cleaned. What did it mean?

It was all just background noise to my memories of her.

* * *

A million voices clamoured in the fairground of my dreams and I looked up at an alien sky—so many stars, a scattering of tawny moons—I rode a carousel of fire and my cheeks stung with the bracing speed of it all. Faster and faster.

Their touch when it came was subtle but urgent. I felt the whisperings of voices and the offering of knowledge.

They've been seeding our galaxy for eons, linking all the sentient races that they have found. This fairground is one meeting place of many: the shore of an ocean of consciousness. And I sense it in the background, the liminal rumblings of a trillion minds.

The carousels stretched out of sight. Not all the occupants were human. Not all the carousels contained horses, but rather a menagerie of the familiar and the utterly foreign, dragons, demons, and butterflies.

In the distance I'm sure I saw her. Impossible they assured me, she died before the machinery could take effect. There are no ghosts here. I turned and for an instant saw her face reflected in the polished brass of the carousel.

"In dreams she will always haunt me," I murmur. And I feel their gentle amusement.

Dream? This is no dream.

* * *

Two in the morning and a whole city wakes. A whole continent. As one we walk from our houses. I wave to my neighbours. The Patersons wave back.

"Is this really happening?" Tony Paterson asks.

"Yes," I say. "Yes."

"Then everything has changed."

"Has it?" My eyes widen. "I suppose it has."

The mood is one of celebration. We stand and stare at the heavens and the stars that drift and spiral, bound by a carousel as big and simple as the universe itself.

I close my eyes and feel the touch of countless minds, beyond the brute mechanism of the universe.

No ghosts, they say. Perhaps that's true, but in my heart I feel her. Cannot forget.

The sky above burns brightly, never seeming more mysterious, never seeming more filled with promise. There is so much to learn, but I do not care. I whisper her name and, for a while, that is enough.

A WOMAN IN A QUANTUM UNIVERSE, IN A POOL OF LIGHT, SMOKES A CIGARETTE

He's late.

Her fingers are like birds, flitting, always moving. She likes it best when they find a humming pause against his skin, or follow the simple ritual of lighting a cigarette. Some addictions are rituals; some rituals are stronger than nicotine. Their lies in repetition, in the comfort and the circular meaning that they give to events, even moments as banal as this.

He's late—as he always is—to pick her up. Though not through any laziness or paucity of concern, but because he is like that, set fifteen minutes out of sync with the rest of the universe. She'd tried to explain it to her mother once, laughingly. "It's like his internal clock has found its own weird daylight savings. He's constantly astounded by the time."

As he is. She sees it often in his face, the sudden widening of eyes, the slow shaking of his head—why am I always late?

She smiles.

She always feels an odd melancholy here, standing, smoking, suspended in jaundiced amber; the light haloed by insects given the aspect of stars.

The narrow heaven of this narrow, chitinous cosmos is lit with constellations that swarm.

If you sped up the galaxy that is how it would look. Stars tumbling and spinning like insects, around and around, a close clustering at the heart. Close, though, is only relative, stars move unimaginable distances apart and even these insects rarely touch.

Particles of smoke drift about her, within her. Even when her hands find rest against his skin there is space. Tiny, but when compared with the distance between atoms—themselves made up of vast distances of space—huge.

Perhaps the only place two people can meet is in their thoughts. Not often, rarely, rarely, maybe only once or twice a lifetime. An epiphany shared, sentences colliding.

Something shifted subtly in her universe the day she met him, things unwound, uncurled, swiftened and raced. Fifteen minutes later it happened to him.

That people touch at all in a world where touch is such an oddity, where fields warp and weave and make semblance of touching, fills her with awe.

The headlights of their patchwork Corolla break her reverie. Here where traffic wardens are quick to pounce, she must react quickly, pick up her bag; break the surface of that pool of light. She shakes away her thoughts like water from her hair, drops the cigarette to the concrete and grinds out its light with the toe of her shoe and hurries to the car and its own pool of light, momentarily fused to this one.

Lips touch.

"Sorry I'm late."

"How was your day?"

"Okay, and yours?"

The car pulls away from the light, a cigarette stub smoulders. Insects circle. Circle and burn. The stars above, so much faster, so much slower—do the same.

CLOCKWORK

"Horologe, I'm dying."
"No you're not, Mr Nod. I—"
"Don't you look at that watch! Don't you DARE look at that
watch."

Horologe 18—Razors and Rivers

The light comes on. Ashley's caught me at it again. Her lips purse with disappointment and I cannot meet her gaze nor stop the flush creeping up my neck and across my cheeks.

The pencil in my hand is slick with sweat. Sweat has streaked the page I'm working on, though I'd not noticed until then. Even in the dark I can draw the citadel, just as I can feel it hundreds of kilometres away, across the State border; my dreadful Mecca. The paper is laid out on the desk. The different clock faces given their—now smeared—time relative to their companions.

"It has to stop, Michael. You have to stop doing this."

"I don't know if I can." The pencil snaps, digs into my hand, but fails to break the skin, even in this I am not up to the task.

"Then see someone."

"Who? *Who* can I see?" I realise I am raising my voice. One of the kids stirs.

Ashley's touch, when it comes, is light, and her kisses soft, hesitant, then stronger; lingering, almost catching me.

I pull away.

"Not now. I'm nearly done, it's almost finished."

But we both know I am not. The final *Horologe* is as far from completion as ever, stalled on a moment, as I am stalled.

I look into her eyes and see not hurt but clocks, second-hands dancing, racing, winding down.

"Where are you?" she whispers. "Where have you gone?"

We both know the answer. I grit my teeth and smile. "Not now, my love. I don't have time. I . . . "

Ashley, patient Ashley. She puts a finger to my lips, draws me close. I know this dance, but I am awkward at first. She holds me tightly and I can feel her tears on my neck, an accusation, an outpouring of love.

"I have an idea," she says.

* * *

We pulled into the lookout, and it rose above the engine noise, invaded the silence that filled the car; whispered damningly in my skull. Even in the car park, at least a kilometre away from the citadel, the great machinery could be heard, its ticking clear.

Ticking, yes, but such ticking. It contained far too much of the clicking of crickets or the dry scrapings of bones. Though I was later to have a more intimate knowledge of its gears, escapements, balances, main springs, palettes, and wheels through schematics in popular mechanical magazines—bought guiltily as though they were porn—that was how I always imagined the sound; nothing mechanical about it, just the dry insectile rasping of bone upon bone.

"Stretch your legs?"

Dad's voice was odd, his eyes slightly unfocused. It was the first time he had spoken since we had started driving.

I nodded and got out the car.

The air was heavy with the fragrance of shadows, of fields given over to moon and stars. Night was coming and the citadel seemed to call it on.

This was long ago, when I was five, predating the citadels transformation into a fetishistic and kitschy tourist destination. Before anyone had even considered constructing a Giftshop of Time or the Chronometrical Museum. Before everything was branded and logofied. Not even a single streetlamp to disturb the coming evening with the gaudiness of light.

They had yet to tar these roads or even bother over-much with grading them. The drive was long and dusty and everything was possessed with the kind of hyper-reality that precedes a migraine.

My head ached and my stomach was knotted with a bilious vertigo soon to uncoil—and violently—but I couldn't tell my father.

I really didn't know what to say. We were a collection of silences even then.

Mum had always spoken for us. But she was dead and I felt sick and we were here and I didn't know why.

And I don't think Dad did either.

We looked into the valley filling up with night and then something shuddered within my father. I stared up at him and watched a shadow cross his face, a deep grief indistinguishable from cruelty.

He picked me up and put me on his shoulders and walked towards the concrete steps leading down into the valley.

And with every stride the clocks grew louder, and the stars spun sickeningly above me in time with all that ticking. I struggled for a while, finally giving up; my head ached too much. Simply blinking made me nauseous.

We descended. Down into the valley. Down into darkness and across the valley floor until we were next to the citadel. Until all I could hear were the clocks. My heart pounded, trying to match a cacophony of time.

Dad pushed my hand against the metal and I felt it as I heard it. Clocks, cold and restless and hungry. Creatures caged, but caged inadequately.

Dad lowered me to the ground and walked away and something hanging from the nearest buttress brushed my head.

* * *

The Clockwork citadel was built during the Depression and finished on the eve of the Second World War, when countries had tumbled to madmen and old leaders wept and realised how badly they had fared. The citadel's architect, Malachy Van Nurrish, an eccentric millionaire, hanged himself that night, from the Western buttress—a spider leg of steel spanning half the valley. A minor player in the League of Nations, he could not bear to see it come undone.

I don't think there is a more wonderful piece of work, at least not in the Southern Hemisphere. A sizeable chunk of Van Nurrish's millions were used in its construction. The finest craftsmen from Germany, Austria and Switzerland were employed.

And they made a marvel. I have spoken to engineers and every one of them agrees that it could not be built today; the art and craft of the thing is lost and such horology is beyond us.

Einstein's theories of relativity were a little over thirty years old and they had gripped Van Nurrish like a madness.

Time is not static but fractured and warped, dependent on so many factors. None of the clocks on the citadel ran to local time. Some ran faster, others slower. On the Eastern wall there is a clock that will take over a thousand years to make a circuit, barely three minutes have passed since its assembly.

In sunlight it is the colour of rust—that thousand-year circuit would, in all likelihood, never be completed. A great iron edifice from which project five spiralling buttresses and at the base of each, and all over the tower, are clockfaces, each declaring a different time from its siblings and none of them correct.

For none can be correct. But, then again, none are actually incorrect either.

I have only seen it once and still it marks me. All that noise, all that ticking. And still I can feel it, sense it against my skin; from that multitude of weathered casements time passes, washes out on to the world.

And it cannot be stopped.

* * *

I started writing comics when I was ten, and he was there from the beginning.

Mr Time, the Chronoman and, finally, Horologe. I filled dozens of scrapbooks with his adventures.

At first he had been an avuncular old man, guiding his companion, Mr Nod, in their battle against crime. But then Mr Nod died and Horologe transformed into something darker, colder. His watch would mark out the minutes to his opponent's destruction. In his eyes the very world ran down and time and death became his enemies.

I don't know what Dad thought of it, he never told me. But he tolerated my dreams as long as I kept at my schoolwork and I got up at four to help him move the cows to the milking yard from paddocks that wore their mist like tattered rags.

When I sold my first strip to a fanzine called *Martyr* and, a few months later, convinced the editors of a metal zine called *Archole* to give me a semiregular spot, I think Dad was proud.

Horologe with his dusty black hair, his gaunt and tired face—eyes haunted and heavy with loss.

His secret hideout was, of course, based on the clockwork citadel.

* * *

"What is time, gentlemen, but decay? And your plans are run down. Just like this WATCH."

"Horologe, TIME is all I need to play this out."

"And time you shall NOT have."

"And yet it is TOO LATE. Your wife is dead. Ah! Do I see a slight tick of emotion there. Has the Hanging Man made you cry.

"I KILLED her and even you cannot turn back the clock, and should you, could you, it would still already be TOO LATE for you.

"In your HEAD you will have always failed her. Whatever happens now, her death is the CAUSATION of it all. A knotted ROPE twisting in your mind. Time must have a beginning, don't you think, and what is better than my beautiful wickedness?"

"Horologe, this TIME I have won."

Horologe 29—Causation Agents

"It's what, a seven hour drive?" Ashley's eyes shine with this sudden conviction.

We can't go there. I can't.

"Yes." But in my mind it is a flickering of eyelids away: a ticking beacon waiting to pour into my head.

"We've got to go there."

"And when do we have time?"

"Now, we are getting in the car. Right now and we are going."

Such impulsiveness. I have to say yes.

"No."

Ashley's lips tighten.

"Not this time." She grabs my shoulders and shakes hard. "We are going *now*. This has to stop. You'll never finish until you face it."

I smile weakly. "You drive first."

"Then you wake up the kids."

They are excited, of course. I pile them into the back of the car.

We're on the highway in half an hour and at this time of night it's as though it was made for us alone. In the dim light I stare at Ashley. My wife is so beautiful.

Her face is etched in my mind and I know its lines and dips. I've sketched the curve of her chin a thousand times, I've felt the weight and light of her eyes, and know all of their possibilities. Or think I do until she suddenly surprises me with something new. And now it is strong with resolve, with a purpose I can only marvel at.

* * *

But I lie if I say I have never been there since. Some places you visit in dreams again and again. Some places visit you. Fourteen and it found me.

I stood knee deep in grass, brittle, yellowing, summer grass. The citadel rose above me, its clockwork beat roaring in my head; gears and wheels rumbling, ticking, tocking, groaning under the weight of all that time.

On the furthest buttress from me, though I dare not look, I knew he would be there, a single figure hanging, broken-necked, spinning in short circles, dancing on the dry hot wind.

And because I was doomed, because the dream was a tide and inevitability, I walked towards the citadel.

When I was near, so close that I could almost touch it, the ground shook and the brass doors at the tower's base flung open like the wings of an iron dragon and I stared into the guts of the machine.

What I saw was all gleaming carapace and legion, and it came pouring out. A cloud of razor-jawed insects, their wings beating in time with the clocks. And on the dry wind they raced—hungry as time is hungry—towards me.

I woke, my bones rattling in my skin, my heart clenched and stung with adrenalin.

And I was shuddery with the realisation that I would die. That my life was finite and my heart would beat only so many times.

I pulled myself out of bed and staggered to the mirror and my murky reflection there. My body was lean, my arms smooth, but in the half-light of night, everything was grainy, like an old photograph. Everything was drained of life and I could not see my eyes, just the bare outline of a face that in the dark could be anyone's.

In my coffin, I thought, it would be darker than this and the darkness would melt my features and I would not know peace, just nothingness. Nothingness forever. Filled with that cold, unspoken inevitability, I sat down, cupped my face in already hardening hands and cried.

Four o'clock in the morning, in the greasy, uncertain light, I worked with Dad. And we worked in silence.

I wanted to ask him, to tell him everything about my dream, about the cruel truth gripping me.

But I didn't say a word.

* * *

It's simple really.

I am always in that car, on my way back from the citadel. And Dad is always beside me, driving the car in his capable way. And though we can't talk, it doesn't matter. And though Dad left me alone in the dark, we are here now and the citadel is a hundred kilometres behind us.

For a few years, at least Dad's are perfect.

On the way back—my head full of ticks and tocks and the world narrowed down to the space between the headlights and the green, radioactive glow of the dashboard—we almost hit a roo.

Dad swerved and slid momentarily out of control. But he was Dad and he brought the car out of its fishtail. I looked back and the roo was standing in the middle of the road, oblivious to how close it had come to death.

* * *

I left the farm when I was nineteen. It ate Dad up, but he did not say a word. Just wished me well as we sat on the porch, drinking beer and looking over all I had turned my back on.

"We've got some good hands on now. But you'll be missed by some of the younger ones. You'll be back for Christmas?"

"Yeah."

But I was back much sooner than that.

Dad did not last the year. I can picture him there in the quiet of his room, looking over the test results one more time. Did he think about time, did he think about it running down?

He put the gun to his lips and . . .

Dad had left me a note. Simple, straightforward. And as maddeningly enigmatic as he was.

Goodbye.

I hadn't even known he was sick.

I sold the farm, I could not bear to face the ghosts it held. I thought it would be enough.

* * *

Ashley is driving and, guiltily, I fall asleep. A dream finds me. I am sure it was following the car, waiting for this moment, waiting for me to fall into it.

I am in a bathroom the colour of a migraine, alone but for footsteps fading away. I call out, no one responds and soon the footfalls are gone.

Something is ticking. The noise hurts my head, filling me with such terrible pain that I have to find it. I open the first toilet stall door. Nothing. The second one, and yet again, nothing.

One by one, I open the doors until I get to the last. The ticking grows louder. I am certain the source of my agony lies behind this door. I take a deep breath and kick it open.

The stall is empty.

Then I taste blood. I cannot breathe; my throat is tight with fear.

I cough, dislodging an enormous clot that shatters on impact with the white tiles.

Then the floodgates open and I fall, retching onto my hands and knees.

Blood. There is more, surely, than one body can contain, but it is all mine. And I see the blood for what it is: thousands of tiny cogs and wheels.

Clockwork.

* * *

There is money to be made in anything, if you are industrious, if you possess a certain talent and a lot of luck. Horologe never made me much, just enough to live off—which, believe me, in this industry *is* a lot. He also gave me a certain reputation.

I wore my black leather jacket, attended just enough cons to keep the work coming and ghosted my way through the nineties.

And selling the farm gave me enough money to not have to worry about much financially.

I met Ashley at a con. I don't think she had read a comic in her life. She worked at the Brisbane Convention centre and we bumped into each other at a café. Literally. By the time I had wiped coffee off my jacket, and gotten up, red-faced, to help, I was already offering to buy her another and she was already saying yes.

I ducked out of two panels that evening. We both loved *The Pixies*, our favourite movie was *The Wizard of Oz. I* thought she was beautiful and she laughed at my jokes.

We were dating seriously by the end of the month. I proposed within six.

I had never been so certain about anything in my life. I never wanted kids until I knew her.

My sketchbooks were littered with clocks and the spiny form of the citadel. But I could hide it as work; Horologe's base and then the Tickers in my children's books.

But such obsessions cannot be hidden for long; the greater the subterfuge the more fragile the secret.

When Ashley first walked in on me drawing the clockfaces, over and over, I felt guilty as though she had caught me masturbating.

"What are you doing?"

"Drawing. This, it's what I do when I can't think. It calms me. Keeps the writer's block at bay."

Ashley smiled, but it stopped at her eyes as she reached for a tissue and put it to the side of my face. It came away wet.

I brought my fingers up and touched my damp skin, had I been drooling or weeping?

* * *

"Ticking, tocking, counting down. How long did it take you to walk these halls?" asked Ticker 7.

"Twelve minutes," Edmund said, not understanding how that would help him find his father.

"Ho Ho! Ha Ha! That's where humans always fail. Twelve

99

*minutes and five point two seconds. You'll never be a Ticker,
Edmund, if you ignore the seconds and all gradations of."*

"That's why I need the Timepiece."

"And that's why we will help you!"

The Twelve Tickers of Tasmania

I don't see the roo until the last minute, because all I can think
about lies two hours in the future. It is a creature sprung whole
out of the darkness, conjured up by my headlights, and all I can
do is swing the wheel sharply to the right.

Tyres squeal, lock up and, for a moment, the wheel is a dead
thing in my hands.

A moment pinned on forever, until I'm back in control, and
the roo is past and both of us are lucky to be alive. I glance in the
rearview mirror, but the night has already claimed the creature.
There are nothing but shadows behind me.

I take a deep breath, slow the car right down and look over at
Ashley. She's opening sleep-heavy lids. From her obvious lack of
reaction, I'm not even sure if what happened actually happened.

"Not far to go now."

She pats my leg and falls back asleep.

"That was close," a voice says, from behind me.

"Yeah, don't tell your mother."

"Tell mum what?" Ashley asks.

Chris yawns. "Nothing. Just boy stuff."

I wink into the rearview mirror.

"Yeah, just boy stuff," I say.

* * *

And it just kept getting worse. Every day I would catch myself
drawing the clocks. Every night the citadel would come to me in
my dreams. And the happier I was the more terrible it became.

I had a woman I loved, and two children, two wonderful children and all I could do was wonder how long we had. How many minutes there might be left to us.

When Confluence Comics picked up the Horologe series for twenty more issues, it made it worse. I hooked them with the promise that by the end, Horologe's journey would be done, and they would own a small piece of comic book history.

I had to finish the series. I had to do something else, but I couldn't. I couldn't find an ending, only clocks. Clocks running down, deadlines that I couldn't get a handle on.

And like father, like son. I couldn't say a word, just drifted further and further from my family.

* * *

The gravel growls as we pull into the lookout, and there below us is the citadel. Everyone is asleep, morning is still little more than a murk in the sky and I pull the car to a very gentle halt.

I stare at my family, sleeping, then down at the tower. I'm out quickly, shutting the door quietly behind me. And then I can hear it.

The citadel is a plug of darkness below. The power must be out but, then, I knew it would be. I don't even notice until his hand is in mine.

"Dad?"

Something hangs from the Western buttress, down where I had stood as a child, in the dark abandoned to time. It could be a banner torn free by the wind or it could be a man.

"Dad?"

He grips my hand tightly and begins to lead me to the steps. Mutely, I follow.

Down we go, into the ticking, unabated for thirty years. Sinking into time.

Before I know it, we are there.

"Here's what you wanted. Here's what you're afraid of."

I look down and realise that the kid is not Chris. I look down and see my own six-year-old face. I push my hand against the metal and it is throbbing and hungry. Something brushes against my shoulder.

A foot. Van Nurrish stares down dead-eyed and then the doors swing open, the great doors at the front of the citadel and I see it all. The clockwork, the machinery of time and of death. And for a moment I shake, but I am not the boy I was. I am a man. And it has taken me all this time to realise that. I face the emptiness, stare at it, not with horror or anger, just resignation.

"Go," the boy me says. "It's waiting for you."

He tries to pull me to the door and I easily turn away.

"No," I say.

And it is enough.

Dawn is breaking, spilling out over the hills as I reach the car and wake my family.

"How long have we been here?" Ashley asks as they get out.

"Not long," I say.

Chris races to the rail, Ashley yells at him to walk. I pull Jessica from the car seat. She's a little weepy at first, but she snuggles into my shoulder

The clocks are ticking down below, echoing as clearly as they have ever done in my mind.

I walk over to Chris. "What are you thinking?"

Chris looks up at me. "It sounds like a thousand typewriters going at once."

"I wish I'd thought of that."

Chris looks at me.

"Dad, are you alright?"

"Yeah, I think I am." I hug him tightly.

Did Dad ever love me? I'm not sure, except he hurt me in the way only those who love can.

We walk down to the citadel.

For a moment I think the doors will open again, but they do not. For a moment I imagine the clockfaces shaking in their casements, straining to drown me in their substance.

And maybe they do, but it doesn't matter.

For this is what matters.

Ashley kisses my neck. Jessica is staring up at it in rapt fascination, until a bird rifling through a nearby rubbish bin catches her gaze, then she doesn't give the tower a second thought.

Chris touches the nearest section of the tower, a tiny clock is right next to his tiny fingers. I reach my palm over his hand. Here is cold iron and warm fluttering flesh. And they are not alike.

"Dad, what does it do?"

I smile, pull his hand from the iron and hug him. "It tells the time, just not very well."

* * *

"Would you know the moment of your death? I can tell it to you."

"And to what purpose?"

"Ah ha. You understand. Each minute is the same, is it not? The finer the timepiece, the more identical those minutes grow. I can tell you the moment of your death. Indeed I can measure the length of your life."

"But only I can live it."

"Yes, people are the opposite of clocks. Time is meaningless. We give it meaning. Each minute is a clone of the one that precedes it and the one that follows. But we make them different."

"The moment of my death signifies nothing, except that I have lived."

"You finally understand. You've a life out there, man. Now go, live it."

Horologe 120 Final Edition—Chronos' Captive

GIRL IN A BLACK DRESS

I met a girl in a black dress at the end of a tunnel at the end of the universe.

She was startled by my presence. But then I need only look in a mirror and I am startled by what I have become. The war is an aggregation of unkindnesses, of distortions and woundings.

There was little I could do to reassure her, but smile and wait until her elegances were satisfied I was unarmed.

Neither of us was meant to be here; the place was closed to the public at night. But there are ways and means and old soldiers (and beautiful women) have a knack of getting what they want.

She leaned against the rail and I marvelled at her big dark eyes and the sweep of her shoulders and I wanted to draw her.

Then and there.

A girl in a black dress at the end of the universe.

"I couldn't sleep," I said. "What's your excuse?"

She smiled and pointed to the roil beyond the rail. "That provokes restless nights."

It's hard to ignore the end of the Universe and knowing that it exists simultaneously in the distant future and down a long tunnel under the city is a madding seed in your mind.

For everything is now. There is no beginning, nor end, just consciousness skimming across eternity, sealing up each moment and putting it in its place. And now I stood and stared at the universe cold and endlessly ending beneath a city just two centuries old.

Such wicked cicatrix has this war created, even here on this distant periphery.

"I think I should know you," she said.

"Perhaps. Do you come here often?"

"Not that often, only when I can't sleep." Her dark eyes drew me in. "The universe is a cruel place."

I nodded.

"Crueller than we should ever know." And I remembered the Garden Worlds and the Death I planted there. What genocide that harvest. We each did our bit. And I wondered at the honour in it, at our devotion to destruction, at the unholiness of survival.

I hung my head a moment, to hide my tears and when I looked up, she was still the most beautiful thing I had ever seen.

"Can I draw you?" I asked and she nodded.

And I sketched her. Then and there. And for a moment, a perfect, eternal moment, there was no cruelty; there was no death.

Just my machined hands and the sound of my pen as I drew a girl in a black dress at the end of the universe.

SISYPHUS DRINKING

"You ever going to leave, Michael?"

"One day."

Tomas laughs; big belly laughs. It's the same old conversation. The one we have every time, a sort of ritual.

Only this time I don't remember coming here, but mornings are like that, and a day like today can melt away memories as easily as it turns the roads to soft toffee.

He sets the coffee down before me, as well as one of those rich chocolate muffins—the kind that looks so tempting behind the glass, but always makes you feel slightly sick and very guilty when you've finished.

"I didn't order that."

He ignores me.

Sisyphus, where the bottomless coffee is only a dollar, but it always ends up costing you so much more.

Brisbane in summer has the heat of a Tennessee William's play, with all the passion boiled out, and *Sisyphus* with its air conditioning is a delicious comfort. The coffee here is dark and bitter and truly bottomless. Just when you think the cup is empty it's full again, hot, black and defying reason.

"The city, she's got her hooks in you, and that job, what do they pay you?

"I know what they pay you."

"Just waiting for something better."

"You'll be waiting forever."

My turn to ignore him.

The air is cool and tangy with the eccentricities of Brisbane; espresso coffee; perfume; sweat, and fine tangles of smoke. I bring my lovers here. At first they complain then, with them as well, it becomes an obsession. A third of the clientele I have slept with, fractured romantic journeys begun here, talk all hyped up on caffeine, eyes as sharp as pins.

Sisyphus is the hub of my existence. I did not drink coffee before I came here, before I left my hometown and my safe, small town heartbreaks. I did not even find the smell appealing. Then She brought me here.

I flick through the papers, always a day or two old, check the employment section, find an interesting job—the sort of thing She wanted me to do, something that put my qualifications to use. A quick call on the mobile reveals that it is taken. The muffin tastes great; I fold the newspaper and drop it beside me. In the interim, someone has topped up my coffee; a little tear of milk spins in the umbral whirl of the cup.

I wave to Tomas.

"No more after this."

"Sure."

I always bring a book to read. I like reading in a cafe. Coffee, book—and this time, muffin—simple little intellectual comforts. I like the idea of reading in a café, but I never get more than a page read. I'm always too anxious, always waiting for something. Some revelation, some startling visitor, some current lover, some thing to arrive. It seldom does but the coffee drinking, the caffeine rush, creates an anticipatory hunger, a restless ache.

I wish that I could do this forever, that I had time to sit and read and drink and watch the world drift past the window. But life is not like that, so, instead, I sit and drink, all too aware of time rushing by, that the moments, the loves, the conversation and the books are all too fleeting. Nothing lasts forever, except, perhaps, the perpetual top ups at *Sisyphus*, destined to outlive the heat death of the universe.

"You going out tonight?"

"It's a weekday, Tomas."

"Every day's a week day. That's why the coffee's so strong here."

I glance at my watch.

"I really should get going."

"Finish your muffin. I cook them myself, you know."

"But I didn't even order it."

Tomas is gone. I smile. I love *Sisyphus*. The coffee is cheap; it makes the idea of paying for a muffin that I didn't order seem okay. I gulp down the rest of my coffee and stand up. Only I can't, my legs are stiff; there is no sensation there. I look down at my cup and it is full again.

Oh well, another coffee isn't going to hurt. Not here.

Someone from a nearby table starts quoting poetry. A little Robert Frost, some Kenneth Slessor, all about sleepy towns and schooner bees and the tolling of five bells.

"Tomas, I can't remember coming here."

"You're always here, Michael. Hey, when are you going to leave?" He tops up my coffee.

Poet guy has moved onto Dylan Thomas and the sparing of angels and madmen and good nights and gentleness unwanted. Someone opens and shuts an umbrella; if it rained this morning it didn't cool anything down, only added to the humidity.

Outside, the traffic along Elizabeth Street has slowed to a crawl. The back-packed, garish overflow from the Queen St mall, stumble by. No one comes in. Unless you work in the city, or spend a lot of time here, these places are invisible, dingy, without charm. Some revelation is at hand and the coffee swirls, all bitterness down my throat until I remember that I like sugar and shovel in three teaspoon's worth.

A moment of hyper-melancholy and I call Her—though She's long past anything like I want her to be.

"Hello."

"It's me."

"Who is this?"

"Michael."

"Look, this isn't funny, Michael's—"

The last word is a whisper. It might have been "dead." Damn phone, I always forget to recharge it; the battery light's flashing. It's dark outside. I don't remember night coming on. Some point of transition has been dislodged—like when you go to a late afternoon movie, sun still shining, and come out to stars. I try to get up and fail. Tomas grips my shoulder with his sausage fingers.

"Another coffee, Michael?"

"Do I have any choice?"

Tomas laughs.

"Of course. Of course."

Sisyphus, where the coffee is bottomless.

"Tomas, how long have I been here?"

His brown eyes soften for a moment, and he taps at the left side of his chest.

"A while. A while."

Auden and sanguine frogs leap from Poet Guy's mouth. The coffee is bitter till I add a little sugar, and then it isn't so bad.

Tomas brings over another muffin, macadamia nut and butterscotch. It's still warm and fragrant.

"How much is all this going to cost?"

"Michael, you've paid your coin. That's all."

I nod my head and pick up my book. Time to read. Time to watch the crowds go by. In *Sisyphus* the coffee is bottomless, once you've paid your dollar. Coffee, bitter or sweet, and without pause. In *Sisyphus* I sit, drink, and read and pick at my muffin.

"When are you going to leave?" Tomas asks and I laugh.

"Not for a while," I say. "Not for a while."

WIND DOWN

The ground shook again, a premonitory shuddering that lasted uncomfortably long and stretched up into the sky. Sophie and I exchanged glances as the quake settled down and *Home* apologised for the inconvenience.

"It's going to get much worse," I said and gripped Sophie's hand, maybe a little too tightly because she pulled away. "Do you think, we're ready?"

"No one is ever truly ready." She sounded so tired that I glanced at her quizzically. The dark-brown perfection of her eyes, the crooked twist of her lips.

"What's wrong?"

"I'm tired, Sean."

The faux-sun was dimming for the night and birds were flying home. The air was cooling, gently, gently. Spring, and the wind down was upon us. *Home* was shifting, changing into something that would have no room for us. She whispered in our dreams of her transformation, of the deeper changes that would find their way to the surface in a few days, making it— in a burst of sudden violence—impossible to live here.

Soon it would be just us again.

"We're all tired."

She laughed, and touched my face.

"Oh, Sean, have you ever felt so weary, so damn tired that it's no longer worthwhile?"

My face tightened and I stared into her eyes.

"Yes," I said. "The first time that I lost you."

She cried then.

"Oh, my love, I try to forget."

"Two thousands years and I will never forget. Sophie, memory is all we have." My hand brushed her cheeks, wiped away the tears and brought them to my lips, the taste of sorrow. "When did you morph the tear ducts?"

I looked at her more closely then and realised that she was sweating. A small increase in sensitivity and I could pick up the steady beating of her heart.

"No wonder you're so tired. You're going retro!"

"Yes," she said. "But I was tired before all that. Well before any of this began."

And then I knew. Sean, old Sean, always so slow on the uptake.

I pulled my fingers from hers, stood up and walked away. I did not cry, my body was not engineered for tears—hadn't been for a long, long time.

"I'm sorry. Come back, please."

I barely heard her.

* * *

In Drift everything is ice cold, ponderous and crushing. Logic tells me it's impossible. Sensitivity has been shut down. There is nothing to register absolute zero, just the readings on the virtual screens, just a flickering on the edge of vision that slows to a once a week blink in time with the potential sail's billowing. And what bones I possess are nothing but Cache, but still I feel chilled to them.

The Universe is so damn big and sometimes you Drift and you

Drift alone; and the one that you love is somewhere. Somewhere but not beside you; and the nearest particle is five kilometres distant and no bigger than a skin flake; and still you do your readings and analysis, hoping beyond hope that it is—— faint spoor —and that it's hers.

Empty, big frozen nothing beside the crowding in of your thoughts, and even these are slow and cold, so cold.

I lost her and I thought that was it and then I found her again.

* * *

Sophie caught up with me an hour after the faux sun had turned itself down. Flying by wing, silent so I didn't see her until she was almost upon me. By then I'd had a while to think, to burn and rage.

I'd run to the other end of *Home,* where the small mountains begin, and climbed the nearest one, turning my sensitivity right up, so every foothold and grip burned. Pain became my tears, a mind-numbing release. I'd even reduced my lung capacity, so I lay panting on a ledge when she brought her wing up beside me.

"Sean, this macho bullshit doesn't suit you."

She shivered and I found myself, despite it all, putting my arms around her.

"Cold up here. How did you find me?"

"*Home.*"

"I needed to be alone." As she shivered against me I increased my integumental temperature—to warm her too human skin—and lowered my own sensitivity. "But then, that's what I will be soon."

"Sean, I'm sorry."

"Sorry doesn't make it better."

"I know."

My grip on her tightened. "I don't ever want to let you go."

"But you will, Sean," she said matter of factly. "I'm just so tired and love isn't enough. Nothing is."

We sat there, on the ledge face, looking down towards the village, its lights flickering warmly. Ninety-five people in our clan. Once there were two thousand; things wear out, things wind down.

* * *

"When you were gone, I thought you dead," Sophie said to me. "I thought there was no way that you could have survived."

"I never lost hope."

"But I did. Jesus, Sean, you weren't transmitting; you'd locked up and the stars there were so damn noisy. I couldn't find you. If you hadn't drifted close enough to a star, your systems wouldn't have thawed, you'd still be drifting, frozen and, for all intents and purposes, dead."

And cold, colder than thought, colder than death.

"So I know what it is like to lose a loved one. I know how you will feel."

I brushed her face with my fingertips, felt the roughness of her new-human flesh and wondered how I could have missed this. I was self-involved, so damn self-involved.

"No, you know how *you* felt. I'm not you."

* * *

Home a spinning sentience, a wondrous habitat.

Habitats, what arrogance! Once, long ago, before my race grew tired of space travel, that was their purpose. World ships modelled on cetaceans—deep brained and singing, bellies full of verdancy. But they had changed; abandoned they had remade themselves. Ostensibly they were still harbours of life, but once, where they had merely been organs, recreations of Old Earth environments, now they were sentient and followers of their own paths.

We'd been adapted for space travel, but this was truly adaptation on a huge scale.

We came upon *Home*, and her pod of about twenty—gathered and grazing on the edge of a solar system rich with dust and heavy elements—quite by accident.

Empty, they drifted, as my clan drifted, through the galaxy and beyond. Not sure why, except that it seemed better than an existence swimming on the edge of the Central Deep—the black hole at our galaxy's core.

I have seen the metropolises there, less tangible than smoke, vast as whole systems. Ghosts flit and play and warp and weave. Engines turn and fire. I was given an opportunity to dwell in that intangible empire, we all were. I refused, did not even leave a copy, or a window. I could not bear the thought of parallel lives, of it growing scornful of what I had chosen to do.

Why travel? The laws of physics remain the same in any sector of the universe.

We later discovered we were lucky to find her at all. Her pod was about ready to break up, each to go its own way. She drew us in with old comtalk and greetings.

Why?

She was the youngest of her pod; the only one not truly acquainted with the emptiness of the infinite. She was lonely and garrulous.

Home spun before us and we were welcomed by a puckering of her airlocks and the chatter of an infant.

From the beginning she warned us that it was not forever, that sometime in the future she might change, until then we were welcome to journey with her, to shelter from the cold.

*　*　*

I woke to morning light and looked down into the valley, at the house Sophie and I had made, then turned my gaze across the habitat. The ground swept up and around. Above us *Home's* tiny sea gleamed in the faux-sunlight. A small sailed craft was crossing her, so tiny in the distance and that was nothing to the distances we'd travelled.

Majestic and intimate, we had spent the last two hundred years here. It would all be gone in a matter of days. But, for now, the Faux-sun burned with springtime brilliance and the air was warm and still. I felt Sophie stir beside me.

"Better that this happened when it did," I said. "The planet is suitable, but the core is highly volatile. There is a lot of hard radiation.

"She is a drifter too."

There was no sun out there. We were between galaxies right now. Deep space, empty space, this world burned like a beacon in all that darkness. Like us, she had been ejected from her solar system and cooled down as everything does, even one's fervour for life.

I'd seen the probe's relays, inhabited them for a while, we all had.

Black skies, liquid oceans with a scum of ice. On the major Northern landmass, five huge volcanoes were erupting constantly; the whole continent was sprayed with their ejecta. We could survive there. Rest a while before we began our greater Drift.

Of course, there is a big difference between surviving and living.

Were Sophie to walk on the surface of that planet in her newly morphed form, she would die within a handful of seconds. But she had no intention of ever leaving here.

"Shall we go home?"

Sophie looked at me.

"Yes."

* * *

We'd built the houses to remind us of what we once were. Here we let our defences down and were almost like our ancestors. Our bodies, which, modified, could survive in cold hard vacuum, did not need these places, but something else seemed to.

And soon they would be gone.

Like this palpitating flesh, it was an oddity and a reminder of what had once been so familiar.

There was an air of uncertainty and excitement, as well as, of course, sadness about the village.

Change, things were about to change again.

Only one day to go.

Sophie gripped my hand.

"Scary, isn't it?" I whispered.

"Yes," she said.

* * *

We could all feel it: *Home*'s whisperings and sadness and more than a little fear.

When Sophie slept, I looked up at the ceiling and the shadows shifting there.

"*Home*," I whispered. "She's staying."

"I know, Sean. The universe has worn her out."

"It wears us all down eventually. Change, everything is in constant flux. To stay still takes so much more effort than moving. I'm tired too, just not ready."

"Everything ends, Sean."

"Even love?"

"That's a question for the poets."

"If you're around at the death of the universe, please ask one for me."

Home chuckled.

"If you're there, I might ask you."

"If I'm there."

"I am sorry. I will miss you. But excitement fills me also. Such potential; new networks open up. Knowledge. I wish I could explain, but words fail. I wish I could take you there, to the deep space that I am going."

"We'll find our way."

"Yes. Perhaps, I will be waiting."

* * *

Preparations were completed; new forms more suitable to the nearby planet were grown on the outer surface of the habitat. One by one, we would upload to them, then tumble free.

Sophie rejected my offer to make her a body next to mine. An out should she decide at the last minute that her decision was the wrong one.

"I have made up my mind. I'm not going."

We both knew that she was frightened. That having an escape route would be too hard.

* * *

The last day came and I woke with a sick feeling in the place where my stomach once was.

Sophie lay pressed against me. I gazed at her, stored the image from as many different angles as possible and hurled it deep into Cache. I did not want to forget nor did I want to remember, not too soon.

"I will miss you," I said.

"I know you will." Her eyes were wide and old, human eyes—not the milky-white pools of the Drift or the silver of the first exoskeletons, or even the green and mauves she had toyed with on Callisto, when we were young and fashion was all.

We'd changed so much. My fingers touched hers, gripped

them tightly. Not quite human flesh against perfect recon-
struction.

"Existence has become an addiction for you, hasn't it?"

"Maybe," I said. "I just want to be there for the End."

"And why?"

I shook my head.

"Because I want to know what happens, I want to experience it. Because I am stupid, I don't know."

* * *

Together we watched the last of our Clan leave. With each upload. a body would fall, another humanoid scattering on the village green.

The creatures of the habitat began to migrate, shifting to places where resources were most needed. A flock of starlings flew over-head, to be swallowed by a cliff face. Rabbits melted into the ground, a forest ejected itself into the Faux-Sun.

Though I'd always known every element of *Home* was merely that, it still startled me to see it so obviously displayed.

Sophie took my hand and led me to a shaded spot and pulled me down.

The sun was warm on our skin as we kissed. I switched every-thing but the simplest feedbacks off, felt the grass beneath us, the spring-warm wind. I buried myself in her and she held me, so tightly, so passionately. We made love, over and over again, not saying a single word, just drowning in the depths of each other's eyes—the fears and hopes and endings.

Epiphanies come not too often in a relationship as long as ours. Eons pass and you become reflections. Eons pass and profundities are worn down. And then you say goodbye.

She kissed my cheek.

"You had better go, my love."

"Yes, but . . . " She pressed a finger against my lips.

"Don't spoil this with words. Just go."

I nodded once and she smiled. On that perfect spring day, I looked upon my lovers' face a final time.

Then I discarded my body—left my love to this final change for that was all I could do—let it fall next to hers and woke in the cold of space, my rubbery flesh stinging. My eyes awash with information, stars gleamed chill and distant.

The habitat shivered beneath me. Great knots of flesh burst from *Home's* surface. Areas went hot and cold all over the place.

I leapt from her back and into the void, *Home* spinning slowly behind me.

* * *

Home distorted. I felt the weave of her thoughts tear, unbind and reform. Saw her flicker in the darkness of space and then, with a triumphant cry—all frequencies rang with it—she was gone. A burst of exotic particles the only trace of her departure.

I spread my potential sails and drifted awhile.

I felt tired, worn out, but I had miles to go before I slept.

I would see the End—whatever that might be—and, maybe, my lover's face.

"There's no place like home," I whispered into the cold and followed my clan down towards the planet burning so far away.

A THIEF IS A KING IN THE HALLS OF THE NIGHT

"A thief is a king in the halls of the night
Heigh ho.
The thief is king!"

Yossard groaned and threw his hands into the air. "Well, that's it. I've had enough." He jumped to his feet, somewhat unsteadily, and made for the door. Marisen grabbed his shoulder, pulling him to a halt.

"Why, what's wrong?" he asked, eyes twinkling.

Yossard rounded on him and pointed, with a shaking hand, at the bard performing before them. "That song. Your song!"

"Why, it won a prize, dear friend."

Yossard's face darkened. "In a competition rigged, I believe."

"The judges were honest, once."

"And made dishonest by the weight of gold in your purse. Or was it the bully-knife at your belt?"

"A gentle prompting, a certain highlighting of the song's attributes, all quite acceptable in such a competitive field."

Yossard shook his head. "How much do you pay them to sing that rubbish?"

"Pay! The bardic guild does not charge a fee. It is more of a commission."

"Fee, commission. Bah!"

"Stay, stay; at least for the chorus."

"Damn it, Marisen. I was there when you wrote the song—curse that day. I know the blasted chorus, I know it off by heart."

He stormed out of the Inn.

Shrugging, Marisen followed him.

Yossard's eyes blazed. "Every night. Every night that we go out, sometime, somewhere, I hear that blasted song. When will it end? Surely it has had its day!"

Marisen smiled. "Actually, I am negotiating with the Bardic Guild to have it given classic status."

"Classic st . . . " Yossard's cry of grief was halted by a distant, bloodcurdling howl. Both men shook and stared at one another, faces wan.

"Where did that come from?" Marisen asked.

Yossard pointed north. "Aptly enough, from the boneyard."

He looked up. There were no stars out tonight, and the moon was in shadow. Yossard loosened his sword in its scabbard, watching his friend do the same.

"It is going to be a long night."

Yossard nodded, pulling his cloak about him. "Cold, too."

"Best we go indoors, preferably somewhere with thick walls, a heavy door and a bolt."

* * *

"Could we have more candles, please?" Yossard said. "Tallow, anything, and build up that fire."

The bordello-mistress frowned and pursed her lips in anger.

"Why is my door bolted? Why is every candle lit and every lady left unoccupied?" She tapped her forefinger hard against

122

Yossard's chest. "Oh, please tell me, dear beer breath. And, if you cannot tell me that, please tell me why you have yet to pay last month's bills?"

Yossard grew petulant. "It is not my fault. He keeps on bribing the bards. Marisen, you tell her."

Marisen did nothing of the sort, being far too busy entertaining several women at once with tales of his bravery.

"Please," Yossard rolled his eyes. "Get him to stop or he'll sing that dreadful song of his."

"Which one, they're all dreadful."

"I heard that!" Marisen turned his gaze towards them and the mistress cursed all handsome folk; particularly those of charming and untrustworthy nature. She opened her mouth to speak, and got no further. Something slammed against the door. Once, twice and then . . .

The door, and most of its frame, shot across the room. For a moment, Yossard wondered if the door had decided to destroy itself in preference to hearing Marisen's damn song.

The women screamed, not to mention Marisen, who none-the-less unsheathed his sword. Yossard paled, staring at the figure framed in the shattered doorway, and didn't bother with his sword, except to touch the pommel once, for luck.

"Demon." He breathed, then hazarded a quick glance at Marisen. "Marisen, the women. Make sure they—"

"They've already gone."

Surprised, Yossard glanced around. Sure enough the room was empty. *Trapdoors and secret passages no doubt*, he thought, and wished he knew exactly where they were, so he could slither away from this.

"The women are safe," the creature said, in a voice more snapping bones and bubbling phlegm than vocalisation.

Yossard looked into its eyes, and saw truth and disappointment; not to mention other things that shook a handful of years off his life.

"I am bound and made but for one task," it said.

"And what is that?" Marisen asked.

"You will know soon enough."

Both men had their suspicions, none were very pleasant.

Yossard backed away, until he was next to his companion. Marisen glanced at him.

"Shall we try and fight?" he whispered.

The demon's mocking laughter was enough. Marisen hastily sheathed his sword. Blades and what mean magic they knew would not suffice against its kind.

The demon turned and motioned, with a smoking fist the size of Yossard's head, for them to follow.

So they did.

* * *

What a strange trio they looked.

The gargantuan demon in the lead, ten feet tall, nearly as wide; legs and body the spell-fused and steaming wreck of half a dozen corpses. It stepped, a squat—for all its height—and brooding schoolmaster. Yossard and Marisen followed; chastened students, anticipating the worst caning of their lives.

It led them swiftly down Chalcion Street and Fischeer Lane, past the gallow field, where ropes blossomed with thieves not as skilled nor as blessed as they. Then North, pausing only once, to cock its broad head at the distant sound of pipes and the chant of murderbards, and grin, perhaps, with some dark and netherworldy appreciation.

The lanes and alleys that they took were deserted, the air dense and dark, the few street lanterns and braziers glowed feebly. It seemed this night had chilled and dulled the effulgence of flame. But, even in the darkness, their destination was obvious.

"See," Yossard whispered, nodding Northwards. "The boneyard. My suspicion proves true."

"And what is that?"

"Yon lies trouble."

Marisen snorted; a mocking sound for all the fear it contained. "Your deductive capabilities astound me."

"Silence." The Demon spat—— a tongue or two tumbling from its mouth—and the two men shut up. Or, rather, they switched their colloquy to the fingertalk of the Easlinan folk. A silent language, not at all to Marisen's tastes, there weren't nearly enough adjectives.

If the demon sensed their talk, it did not comment. They walked on in apparent silence.

* * *

In the heart of the cemetery, atop a stony knoll, as the midnight bells rang out the hour and the day—they came to a halt.

"Welcome." The voice was strong, almost melodic. Out of the shadows stepped.

"You," Marisen said.

"Yes, me."

Yossard looked from Marisen to the man—garbed in a wizard's robes—and back again.

"Who?"

"Dimixatren."

"Dimixatren." Yossard said. "Perhaps a wizard we have betrayed—or did we kill his brother or steal some magical . . . "

"No, to them all," Marisen said. "A bard of high repute—and now, as we have discovered, a wizard of low and desperate magics. Some say I stole his title this year in the Bardic contest."

"I knew it!" Yossard growled. "Your damned ballads. No good could ever come of them." He turned towards the bard. "If it makes you feel any better, I think his canon is rubbish, pure and simple."

"No, it does not make me feel any better."

"Can we get this over and done with!" The Demon boomed. "I was attending a performance of the Malacia."

Dimixatren glared at it. "For all that Opera's baleful magnificence. I am the master here, pit dweller. We will do this thing at my pace."

The demon roared at the insult and a dazzling burst of fire crashed at the wizard's feet. Dimixatren did not so much as blink—even Yossard, wincing at the smell of charred, demonic flesh, was impressed by the bard's control.

"I am the master," Dimixatren said again, in a voice quiet and potent.

"So you are," the Demon muttered. "So you are."

"Now," the bard said, turning on the pair. "You are probably wondering why I brought you here?"

Yossard sighed.

"I have a fair idea." He pointed at his friend. "Something to do with him, I'll wager. For the life of me, I can't understand why I'm here at all."

Dimixatren snorted. "I know what your kind are like. Were I to kill your associate, you would seek revenge."

Marisen raised an eyebrow.

"No doubt, he would, for we are as brother to brother," he said. "By cruel cuts and ancient vows our lives are as one."

Yossard glared at his friend.

"Marisen, if we survive this, I will kill you."

Dimixatren laughed.

"Survive, I think not. You see, I was cheated in the bardic prize, but I will not be cheated again. My Ballad of the Adnian Priest was five times five the better of your piece—why I workshopped it in the Bardic Halls to great acclamation. How such popular trash as yours ever . . . "

"I would not go so far as to call it popular." Yossard interrupted.

Dimixatren glared at him. "I was done wrong, and now I

have summoned this demon to be an arbiter—in his world he is regarded as the finest of music critics."

At this, the bulky monstrosity bowed, the misplaced bones and cartilage tissue of its makeshift spine cracking loudly in the still air.

"Music is my life," it said.

The wizard nodded, and his eyes locked with Marisen's.

"Both you and I shall perform our works, and the better man lives and the worst, well, the worst is bound to hell for eight to nine eternities of agony. Tonight, dear opponent, while the heavens are dimmed and the umbral moon holds court, we sing for our souls!"

"An interesting idea," Marisen said. "But for one thing. I am a lyricist not a performer, who will sing my piece?"

* * *

"Oh, no, you don't!" Yossard's face was hot. "This is too much. I can't."

"If you do not, you forfeit the contest." Dimixatren nodded at the demon, its brutal face stretched with a hungry grin—and the attendant crackings and soughing of mismade flesh. Hell burned in its eyes and, momentarily, Yossard thought, he could hear the distant cries of the damned. The damned didn't sound like they were enjoying themselves all that much.

Yossard back-tracked rapidly.

"You've made your point. I will sing, for all the lyric is ash in my mouth. I will sing so that our souls escape the lash of Demonic torments." He turned and jabbed a finger at his friend. "And you. You will pay for this! By all the blasted gods in heaven and all the demon princes of hell, once I am done, I'll tenderise your skull. Perhaps the flat of my blade will work some sense into that dullard's brain of yours."

Marisen made to protest, thought the better of it and smiled weakly back.

Dimixatren nodded.

"The rules are quite simple. I will sing my ballad and then you. And on the completion of your song, the Demon will bring his judgement to bear."

"How do we know you won't cheat?" Marisen asked.

Dimixatren seemed shocked.

"What kind of lowlife do you take me for? I am a Bard. My word is iron. Should my song be judged the inferior, my shields of protection will fold and the Demon shall have me." Dimixatren turned to Yossard. "Are you ready?"

The tall thief's face was grim.

"Let it begin," Yossard said.

Dimixatren began, wasting no time, and with absolute confidence.

He sang—in a voice of richest honey—a piece of such subtle intricacy, sadness and joy, that in places Yossard was moved to tears, then great bellows of laughter.

Twice, he turned to Marisen and exclaimed—though with sinking heart:

"Now this. This is music!"

Marisen meanwhile listened intently, face a-frown, murmuring, on occasion, to himself—though with any veracity of musical knowledge or just a desire to distract it was uncertain.

"Missed a beat there. My God, he's mixed his metaphors again."

When the priest was laid to rest, the children of the Copper King paraded by, and a Dragon slain, in a surprise and stirring climax, by the beggar prince with the leprous hand (leading to his untimely demise, crushed in the Dragon's death throes, then resurrection as the Priest's successor).

Yossard knew that they stood as good a chance of winning as a candle burning steady in the Chamber of Storms.

"Marisen. Marisen, I hate you," he whispered, wiping tears from his eyes. "He writes a song for our times, potent, dark and joyous; as labyrinthine as our city's streets. You write a rollicking, senseless drinking ballad. Damn you to hell."

Marisen looked at his friend sternly. "If you do not sing, you will do just that. Dare I say it, you will damn us both to hell."

Yossard sighed deeply. "Yes, you are right."

He bowed his head a-moment, then began to sing.

In his heart of hearts, Yossard considered himself a wonderful singer, and that if thievery had not claimed him, he would have claimed the love of all with the melodic voice of an angel.

One's heart of hearts is capable of swallowing the biggest lies.

Yossard possessed a flat and nasal baritone, a rolling and unrythmical style that fragmented and made unrecognisable almost any song. Marisen who had never heard his friend sing before, except when very drunk, felt his jaw drop and his lower spine shudder with a thousand anticipatory screams. He wondered what it would be like to burn forever in the underhell. Soon enough to find out, he thought, burying his face in his hands. Soon enough.

At last Yossard finished—face flushed and almost winningly shy, as he waited for judgement.

Marisen cringed.

There was a flash, a burning sulphurous light and a long and agonising scream.

Marisen stared at his friend. The Demon and Dimixatren were gone.

It was the current, the crossburn of razors and the whisperings of a billion madding, undone scars.

He screamed and screamed again. His flesh and soul the subject of awful agonies, caused by the merest contact with the demonic plane. He felt each cell boil, heard the sizzle of his skull and heart and the crazed unstitching of his soul.

"Why?"

The Demon laughed at him, its voice a serpentine pain within his bowels, and a slithering that coiled and uncoiled in his ears. He felt, endured, rather than saw its amused gaze.

"Because you are brilliant. Simply brilliant. Dear Dimixatren, how could they understand you up there?"

"Brilliant?"

The Demon laughed.

"Don't be modest. Sing!"

Lips uncoiled from Dimixatren's flesh. His eyes hollowed then stretched, a multitude of tongues lashed out, and his body became a hundred mouths, a chorus of pain and horror.

He sang, became song.

And Hell, in all its seething fury, paused to listen.

Marisen grabbed Yossard by his shirtfront and shook, savagely.

"Don't you dare sing my work again."

Yossard grinned, pushed his friend away and danced, arms swinging gracelessly, around the tombstones.

"We are alive. We are alive!"

Marisen was livid.

"Through no thanks to you, that was the worst . . . "

Yossard's eyes shone with hurt.

"Why, I sang my heart out."

Marisen shuddered.

"Aye, you did and it rotted in your throat."

He walked to where Dimixatren had stood. All that remained were two smoking footprints. He looked over at the bard's collection of magical instruments—all high quality stuff.

"Well, these'll make us an iron or two at the market ground—and we do owe our women quite a bit of money. Get me a bag."

Yossard pulled one from beneath his shirt—kept there for

such contingencies—humming a few bars as he did so.

"Damn you," Marisen muttered as they walked from the cemetery hill down towards the waking city, the sun an eyeslit of gold to the west. "How can I ever write another piece again? How can I?"

He did not finish, for Yossard began anew his song, his voice echoing among the worn old stones of the graveyard:

> "A thief is a king in the halls of the night
> Heigh ho.
> The thief is king!"

And Marisen, gnashing his teeth, did not so much as utter a word.

MY BROTHER IS GOD

When I found out that my brother, Denis, was God I was pretty pissed. We'd always been competitive, but two most improved player trophies for soccer and a first in Maths B couldn't top that.

"Why didn't you tell me?" I said as I smacked the back of his head.

"I didn't want you to know."

"Some God you are. We found out anyway."

"Yeah. I stuffed up there."

"So does Dad get to quit his job and we all move into a mansion with a swimming pool?"

"It doesn't work that way."

No, it didn't.

Mum had caught him talking to angels and Dad found the Secret Control Room—in some astounding synchronicity. Putting two and two together they asked him to come to the kitchen—the single, glaring, hundred watt globe (pearl), the uncomfortable cracked blue vinyl and metal chairs, and the laminated, wonky-legged table making our family's equivalent of the interrogation room—and got the truth out of him. I imagined his right eye twitching like it always did when he was caught lying, twitching like mad.

I'd been at soccer training, so I missed it all. Mum was peeling potatoes and Dad watching the football when I stomped in, knees muddy and lungs sticky with cold.

Denis was in my bedroom reading a comic.

"That's mine," I said and Denis nodded.

"So it is."

"Put it down."

"Mum's got something to tell you. I think you should see her."

"Put it down."

He looked up, eyes hard. Denis could be a pretty mean fighter when he wanted to. And, this time, I knew he would make it count. I decided to let it lie and walked to the kitchen instead, mumbling under my breath.

"Mum . . . "

"Terry, your brother is God."

"Bullshit."

Mum stared at me, lips tight.

"Don't swear, Terry, it's unbecoming of a gentleman. Denis is God and you're to love him all the same. We all will." There was a hesitation in her voice and, I think, she almost cried. She strengthened though and smiled and hugged me tight. I was at that awkward age and pulled out of her grip.

"Mum," I groaned. She blinked and laughed a little.

"Not too old for a hug, young man."

The kitchen smelt of dinner and the lavender in my mother's perfume. Denis walked in a little shyly. Mum gave him a hug too. Hugged us both, till Dad called out for a beer.

* * *

I woke one Saturday morning with an angel hovering over my bed, staring at me with eyes of radiant knowing—joyous, loving and filled with contempt all at the same time. I knew he could reach down with his needle-thin fingers and pluck out my pounding heart. Knew that part of him wanted to. I could barely breathe, couldn't move, as he fluttered above me and time grew all slow and cold.

"Malak, no," Denis said and, suddenly, the angel was gone. Denis snorted. "That Malak, he's crazy."

"Why? Why is he like that? He's an angel after all."

Denis shrugged his shoulders. He was reading another one of my comics.

"Good and Evil. Angels exist simultaneously at both extremes."

"And what about you?"

"I'm God," he said smugly. "I transcend everything."

"Transcend this," I said in my best Schwarzenegger accent and gave him a good pummelling. God or no, I could still take him on occasion. It ended with both of us crying—I can't remember who hurt whom, but neither of us wanted to get in trouble—and running to Mum. He got there first. I spent the morning cleaning up my bedroom. Denis taunted me with my comic until Mum got mad at him too. Both our bedrooms were clean by lunchtime.

* * *

One day Denis showed me his Secret Control Room—not so secret any more—out beneath the tool shed.

There were lots of switches and clicking dials and a big blank screen, like out of the old science fiction movies they'd show sometimes on Sunday afternoons—lodged odd and restless between a football match and the evening news. I swear if you looked at that big screen long enough you could see everything. Everything and nothing

"What's all this for?"

"You wouldn't understand. I just use it to control stuff."

"Obviously, but what?"

"CNO cycles, the spin of galaxies. Prime Ministerial Addresses. The Guest Lists of Letterman. You know, just stuff. Most of it's on automatic, but you've still got to keep things moving from time to time."

"Can I have a go?"

"No."

"Why not?"

"Because, you're not God."

"That's not fair."

Denis chuckled.

"God isn't fair. Ask the citizens of Jericho."

He offered to resurrect them for me, one by one and have them explain just what had happened after Joshua blew his horn. He told me it would be easy, not even a miracle, just the windblown fragments of an ancient massacre given new whispering voice.

But I made him stop when the first one began to claw its way out of the tool shed, its bones made of dust, its voice darker, and more terrible than any horror movie creature I had ever scared myself with.

Denis blinked at me, sending it away with a wave.

"That's nothing," he said. "If that scares you, wait till the Parousia. Wait till the end of days, when the clock ticks round to twelve, and see what comes knocking at your door."

I hit him then and he yelled for mum. As I remember it our rooms were very clean that year.

* * *

At first, Mum found the angels difficult to handle. But they seemed to enjoy her company, hovering in groups of threes and fours over the kitchen, watching her cook. She'd shoo them away with a broomstick but they'd always drift back—their wings part silvery-fairy-gloss and cockroach brown—a soft, rustling ambience melding with the kitchen fan and the muttering whine of the fridge.

"Can't you do anything about them, Denis?"

"They listen to me most of the time, Mum. But they're angels. Just like everything else, they've got free will."

In the end, Mum just got used to them. Maybe even liked having them around. She'd slip them the occasional beer or glass of milk. Sometimes they'd even sing for her and I tell you, you haven't heard anything until you've heard an angel sing Sinatra standards or *Hey Jude*. Even I liked it though I would never admit it at the time—I was going through my top forties stage.

* * *

I think Dad was hit the hardest by it all. He'd always been an atheist—and now he had to contend with God in his own house. He and Denis sidled around each other awkwardly.

Sometimes I'd catch him staring at Denis, an odd disappointed expression on his face. If I thought Denis' revelation might have brought Dad and me closer together I was wrong. It was as though one such surprise was all that Dad could take. He didn't want to risk uncovering any other secrets—heaven forbid that I should turn out to be Brahma or the devil or worst of all, gay—so he kept his distance from both of us.

But things continued as they always do—a family is a formidable thing, nearly indestructible in its obstinacy, and there was always mum—football season slid to a close, cricket season started.

* * *

I loved my brother, but it was never easy. He had the rapture, I had my first guilty attempts at masturbation.

They're not quite the same.

"It's not fair," I once said, when we were fishing together. An angel hovered above us; with bored flicks of its wings, reached down on occasion to zap fish then resurrect them; startled and lazarine, they'd flop back in the water and be gone, perhaps to preach to the depths of the miracles that floated cruel and powerful just above the surface.

Of course, with all that going on, we never caught anything.

"How did you get to be God?"

"I just did, I suppose."

"But how did you use the secret control room when you were a baby?"

"I didn't till I was four."

"Then who was controlling everything?"

Denis looked at me from across his fishing rod. His feet were dangling over the pier, his nose was dotted with freckles and reddening with sunburn because, like me, he didn't want to wear his hat.

"Me, through telepathy. You see, in many ways, the secret control room is just a metaphor. It's quite simple, Terry. Stuff usually is."

"What's a metaphor?"

"It's like. It's like, I don't know, I'm just a kid."

"Bet I can throw further than you."

"Cannot."

I could, of course. I was two and a half years older. Threw a stone right across the river. Beat that one, God.

* * *

Mum went to the doctors. She kept on getting these headaches, you see. A few tests were done and they found a tumour in her skull; a quietly growing malignancy, a third and fatal child. Mum blamed the powerlines that ran over our house. I knew it was the angels. Denis denied everything—said the tumour was not the sort associated with ionising radiation—but he kept a tighter rein on them after that.

Mum got sick very quickly, as though, once named, the illness grew all-powerful. The tumour was inoperable. Not a problem though, because my brother was God.

I asked him if he could fix Mum up and he looked at me, quite surprised.

"A lot of people pray to me everyday. To heal this or help with that and I don't do anything. It's not my way. It's not God's way. Why should Mum be any different?"

"But you can change it."

"I can no more change it than you can."

"But you're God. You're everything."

"There are rules. I can't just break them."

"But she's Mum."

"And I am God."

That was always Denis' excuse. He was God. But what kind of God does that?

* * *

One night, after hearing Mum throw up for the eighth time, I could stand it no more. I raced outside, unlocked the toolshed and opened the secret door. The machine hummed in front of me—waiting, all potential, the tiniest of cogs, the smallest, oddest of machines, and yet the great wheels of the cosmos turned at its command.

I gripped the controls and the universe enfolded me and I enfolded it; felt the ballooning endlessness of it all, the odd fracturing and bubbling of things smaller and vaster than my imagining. I tried to narrow it down. Tried to focus on my mother. For a moment, I caught her. For the briefest instant, I felt her love and her pain. Before I could even begin to cure her she was gone from my sights and I knew that I could not bring her back—no more than I could generate a solar eclipse or stir the heart of a mouse. This was God's machine and I was not God. In my rage, I thought to bring it all down, to burst every star, to turn the universe into one blazing rotten scream.

Then Denis was there. His gentleness surprised me as he pulled me—panting, eyes rolling in my head—away from the machine.

"Not for me. Not for you."

"God's will," I said, suddenly feeling so much older.

"Yes."

"Fuck you."

I hit my brother then. Hit him again and again and he let me. Taking each blow until I was exhausted and he was bleeding and on the floor. Disgusted, with myself, with him, with everything, I ran out of the Secret Control Room and didn't look back. I never hit my brother again.

* * *

After Mum died, things fell apart in a kind of endlessly-painful slow-motion—not for Denis; he was God, he had his machinery and his angels—just for the family.

Dad started drinking. He wasn't a cruel drunk, not like some of my friend's fathers, just a sad one. The drink dissolved us from his life. His eyes grew hazy around us, he could not meet my gaze, rarely spoke except when Denis and I were by the fridge, and then it was just to ask for another beer.

I heard him praying once, in the middle of the night, mumbling words to a god that lay a single thin wall away. I stumbled into Denis' room, he was smiling like a cat with a bowl of cream. I left him to his small victory and went back to bitter sleep.

The rest of my childhood played itself out in my room where I read my science fiction books, the roar of innumerable sporting matches coming from the living room television. I said almost nothing to Dad over the next few years I spent at home. Maybe a handful of words.

One of those, at age eighteen, was, *bye*.

* * *

This evening, I ran across Denis at a bar. Surrounded by androgynous types all hungry for belief; as though God could save them.

He'd grown up to be quite a handsome man: black hair, pale skin, neatly trimmed beard—the sort that get invited to all the right parties.

Denis introduced me as his brother.

"I've kept tabs on you," he said to me.

"You keep tabs on everybody," I muttered and he ignored me.

"You've done alright. I like your books, cynical, but with heart."

"If you kept *tabs* on me, why didn't you write? Maybe sent a vision or something."

Denis laughed mildly.

"I stopped doing the vision thing around two thousand years ago—anything after that is pretty much delusional." He looked at me seriously. "You know you weren't ready."

He had me there.

"I don't think I'm ready now."

Denis looked pained.

"Yeah."

An angel startled me, brushing past to whisper in my brother's ear. The rest of the crowd didn't bat an eyelid; maybe they couldn't see it. Faith, after all, was blind. He nodded at its words, before leaning — I'd never seen him look so sad or excited.

"Look. I've got something to attend to. You know, turn of the millennium, Parousia and so on."

"When exactly is that happening?"

"That's for me to know and you to find out. You might see Mum." There was a slight twitch in his right eye.

Ha, but I'd caught him. My brother was always lousy at keeping secrets.

"Tonight, it's tonight, isn't it? Let me guess, twelve on the dot."

His right eye twitched, like it always did when he was caught out.

"That's for me to know and you to find out," he repeated, though I could see in his eyes that he knew that I knew.

He gripped my shoulder.

"Terry, poor, poor Terry. Look after yourself, okay."

Then he was gone.

One of his flock turned to me. She looked stoned. "So, is he really God?"

"You better believe it," I said.

"You're a very lucky man," she said.

"You could say so." I left her to pay for the beer.

Once home, wired and mad, I sat down at the kitchen table, poured myself a drink and waited. The clock ticking, like ants in my blood. 11.59. The End of the world. Parousia.

All I knew was that I hated family reunions. Fuck how I hated them.

The clock struck twelve, and someone knocked at the door.

WILL AND HIS LADY LUCK

Will fought in many wars and survived, not through skill or strength, but blind chance.

Lady Luck was sweet on him: mines would fail beneath his heavy, stumbling shoes, bullets ricochet off his thrawn helmet, and sabres merely part his hair or crack one of the finger-thick lenses of his glasses.

Every war, no matter the outcome, Will survived.

And though he wasn't all that bright, he understood the role his sweet Lady Luck had played.

Understood, too, her capricious nature.

So it came as no surprise that, one day, on the Eastern-most of an Eastern-most front, a bullet tore into his belly and nestled there amongst the intestinal bunches. A leaden, Dear John letter from his mistress that would take hours if not days to read.

All around, his comrades froze, realising that Lady Luck had spurned him and they didn't stand a chance. Sure enough, in a staccato rush of bullets they were dead. Such was the way of this war, where death descended suddenly and conversations would halt, punctuated in blood and bone and brain.

Will lay alone in a bed of corpses, friends turned to silent meat and his own bowel movements turned against him. Peristalsis now a measured tearing squeeze of agony.

"Well. I've had a fair run of it. Sixteen years of this. Lady Luck served me well and, even now, I've time to ponder my demise."

He gazed at the mud and the blood, and the smoke-creased sky. He thought of the cities he'd stormed, a street at a time—no matter what they told you, it was always a street at a time—messy and shattered, pointless death and destruction. Seige engines erupting like storms of iron or trickster gods whose follies were shattered bodies and ironic positionings of corpses.

He thought of a woman he'd once kissed when the last war ran itself out. Thought of the mad scrabble in a dingy room, the taste of her, and he hadn't even had to pay for it.

That was as close as he had come to love.

Except, of course, his Lady Luck.

And now, after the desertion, came remorse.

She stared down at him. He looked up at her face, a visage hook nosed and scarred that—for most—could only be loved in the darkest, most needful times. A face broad, strong, fearful, angry and sorrowful all at once.

"My dear. My dear," she crooned.

Will smiled. "My lady love."

"What have I done?"

"I forgive you."

Near endless battles he had seen. Bullets, poison gas, biochemistries and radioactives that rushed in tsunami clouds. He'd faced them all and survived and killed, and he had outlived every single person he had ever met.

She kissed his cooling face with feverish lips.

And then, capricious as always, she shouted, "A wish. You may have anything you desire."

"Anything?"

"Anything," Lady Luck said. "Hurry, before I change my mind."

Will thought of all those battles, all those terrible wars.

"Then I wish that I'd never been so goddamn lucky."

Lady Luck's eyes widened. Then she nodded.

"So be it."

* * *

They marched onto the stinking field and the bullet struck Will through the eye.

The Sergeant shook his head, reached a rough finger behind the thick lens, and closed the corpse's other unseeing eye.

"First day out and he didn't even reach Vieningrad. Poor boy, Lady Luck wasn't watching out for you at all."

LOOKING BACK

One day out of seven my wife leaves me. Walks from our bedroom, where I lie beneath her framed pictures of Blake's etchings. Cain flees above the bedhead, guilt stamps his face and a kind of mute terror, Newton makes his certain and eternal measurements, body and mind fixed upon the universe's verities.

My wife moves silently and our unit is silent with her. There is no creak of doors or clicking of locks, or footfalls upon the polished wooden floors—which cost us much but not as much as other deals that I have made—not even the fabric of her dress makes a sound. She leaves the unit, walks to the elevator, descends to the ground floor, and onto Albert Street and, from there, to the river. I know this for I am not asleep. I have never slept that night, the night before she fulfils her contract. But then it all grows fraught and perilous that evening. Everything is stilted, truncated, empty and chill; our conversation; our kisses; our lovemaking; and, most of all, our sleep.

When the door shuts, I get up and walk to the window and wait until I see her come out of the shadow of our building, then watch until she's gone. It is unspoken, but I'm sure she knows I'm there. She never looks back, no matter how much I will it. That she might just turn her head towards me, try to glance up at the eleventh story window where I stand and watch her.

My wife is so strong, and in the grace of her steps, and the direction of her gaze —so much commitment —I see everything that I lacked, the failure that led to this. She turns down Mary St and is gone. I make a strong coffee and wait and always there is that odd tumble of memories.

* * *

I do not remember the phone call, or the drive to the hospital. Just her face, pale and bloodless. And the moment of realisation, the bleak and pitiless epiphany.

The doctor was a compassionate soul.

"So unfair," he said. "So very unfair. Newly married?"

I nodded and he tisked, his face twisted with some inner conflict. At last, he smiled painfully, though reassuringly, and pressed two silver coins in my palm and led me to the elevator door.

An orderly was waiting there, his face dark with displeasure.

"This is highly irregular," he said.

"But not impossible," the doctor replied.

"You're nearing your quota."

"I'm a doctor, I don't care about such things," he said airily and left.

But I did.

"What's all this about?" I demanded.

"Press the basement button twice. You'll know what it is and who you are dealing with at once. Everybody does," the orderly said, as though he had swallowed something distasteful. "You better love her."

* * *

The elevator descended, dropped and dropped and dropped; though the lights stopped at the basement, it kept its arduous sinking until I thought it might never end. I stared at my grief-streaked face in the mirrored ceiling—remembering how she had done that, loved to look at her face in the mirror when she was crying. The two silver coins burned in my palm, and I wondered what in God's name was I doing.

Finally, when the elevator stopped and the doors slid open, Death—the orderly was right, I recognised him at once—was waiting for me with a somewhat bemused expression on his pale and rubbery face. His eyes cruel and mocking, yet unfocused. His breath a miasma of medicinal strength alcohol and rot, of things shoddily preserved.

"I'll never understand it." He took my hand in his huge and clammy grip, then pocketed the coins. "Love of your life, eh? Hell is crowded these days, so I'm quite happy to deal."

* * *

When the papers were signed, Death drove me to her.

The streets in that city beneath the sea were quiet, no traffic to talk of but Death's black sedan.

"She's staying at one of the new apartments. Quite nice. Must say though, the buildings lack character. Even hell has succumbed to post-modern utilitarianism—whatever that is. And let me tell you about funding, I don't know where they're allocating money but it isn't down here."

I barely heard him.

"I can't wait to see her. I can't wait to talk to her."

Death coughed significantly.

"Can't do the latter I'm afraid. Dead can't talk to the living, one of those Rules That Must Not Be Broken. You'll have to save all that chattering until you get back."

* * *

My wife was a little odd towards me, which was understandable in the circumstances. Still, we kissed passionately. Her lips cold, but just as soft as I remembered them. I held her hand and led her to the car.

Death's eyes were wide with surprise. "Where do you think you're going?"

"Home."

"You obviously didn't read the small print. It might be easy to get here, but it's a heck of a lot harder to get out." Death lifted an arm and pointed down the street, index finger extended, pale skin, nail black with tomb-mud. "Yon lies the exit."

"Okay."

"Oh, and there is another thing. You cannot look back. A single glance and she will never leave."

"Tough rules," I said, lighting a cigarette and offering him one, which he took.

Death nodded and lit up. He blew half a dozen smoke rings in my face. "I've never been fair, comes with the territory. Surely you don't need me to tell you that."

* * *

We left inner city hell and kept on walking. The place pressing on my skull, persistent and awful, even worse because she was behind me and I couldn't see her.

"You know what I just realised," I said to her. Not sure if she was listening, but speaking none-the-less. "Hell is those ill-conceived dollops of land developments you get on the Gold Coast. You know, brick veneered, nice lawns, but no garden to speak of, every place the same."

I could not even feel her there. The dead make no sound. There is no small talk in hell. Just silence at once profound and meaningless. My voice, rambling on nervously, echoed pallidly in my ears, but I could not stop. Talk was all I possessed, maybe it's all the living possess.

How I wanted to turn to gain some sense of her presence, but I kept my gaze straight ahead. She was an itch at the back of my neck that grew in intensity, became an ache, and then a burn. Was she behind me at all? A single inch, a dozen feet or a mile. There were no footfalls but mine, no breath to wash against my neck. No response to my chatter.

She made no sound, the dead walk silently, the dead do not breathe.

Hell sprawled endlessly. Street after street. In hell it is always three o'clock in the afternoon. Fat bellied men stood on their driveways, with their yapping dogs, and watered their immaculate yards.

Finally, we came to a fence.

"I guess this is it," I said, and hefted myself up, to jump over the other side. I waited there a moment, staring left and right.

Beyond lay a stretch of grass, like the rough on a golf course, and an elevator.

I walked towards it, pressed the button to open the doors and walked inside. The walls were mirrored. I kept the doors open for quite a while, facing forward. We weren't out of hell yet. But I did not see her.

Did I press the button now? Was she in?

And all the while the back of my neck raged. My hair was prickling all up and down my spine.

At last, the waiting too much, I turned around and-

Her eyes met mine, and there was such disappointment in them. And I knew, at once, another truth. The dead do not forget.

Then she was gone.

* * *

Death sighed.

"We're going in circles here. Sorry, but that's it. You signed the papers. You looked back. You weren't supposed to look back." He glanced over at Persephone, raven-haired, dressed in black latex, eyes shadow-rimmed but lit with fire.

"Lawyers, these days can find a hole in every contract," I said.

"He has a point there," Persephone nodded. "Do we really want to tie up half our funds in legal costs?

"Let him have her. You've got that deal with my old man. Four months on, Eight months off. Try something like that on for size."

Death's eyes narrowed.

"Well, it's been good for our marriage. You're lucky we just had that earthquake in LA. Damn place is crowded." He patted my back. "Now got any more of those cigarettes?"

* * *

So we returned to the living and one day out of seven, she leaves me.

We don't talk about it much. We don't talk about anything much. Orpheus tamed Cerberus with his music. I took an elevator down. I wasn't exactly the classical hero, but then Hell isn't what it used to be.

From my window, I watch her walk towards the Brisbane River and the point where it meets the Styx—as all rivers do—just a little past the Botanic Gardens. We don't talk about what she does down there either. I think she might be having an affair. I think she might hate me. All I know is that her kisses are so cold when she returns. And we say I love you so damn often that I can't help thinking of those characters from *Player Piano*.

I asked her once if she could ever forgive me for looking back.

She smiled and laughed. "Forgive you? Of course. I love you, Darling."

She didn't look me in the eye though. I wonder what she would have done in my place. And I know that she would not have failed.

Sometimes, I think that I should follow her, just open the balcony door, step through and clamber up over the rail and then . . .

I do not of course. Six days out of seven isn't bad. And she would not notice.

My wife never has, nor ever will, look back.

ENDURE

After Noon, there is nothing on the Deep Shelf Run, until Carving Mars. Just a road kissed with forever and a fallen down stone keep, built by an eccentric billionaire. The Shelf broke him, as it broke his castle, and a century ago—this T area—the ashlar tumbled, spilled across the road, making it tricky to navigate at night.

The old fortress saddened Margaret. For all its hubris, it had been a dream. She found little cheering about those hopes and stone shattered and scattered across the road.

Worse than that, such a place could not help but be the draw of memories.

When does this end? she asked herself above the hum of the Myartruck's six wheel-engines. And there was no answer. There was never an answer and she had been doing this for so long.

"Here, Margaret." Darwin said, and there was an urgency in his voice that made her turn to him. "We have to stop here."

"But there's still such a long way to go."

"We have to stop here."

Darwin pouted and Margaret brought the Myartruck to a halt.

Margaret humoured him because they were lovers. Damn, she fell in love with every one of them.

"See how our works endure!"

Margaret stared at him oddly, Darwin was always like this, wanting to impress, wanting to astound.

"What?"

"It's a line from a poem by Kipling. Empire Earth poet, wrote his finest work in exile on Europa."

"I know who Kipling was."

Darwin smiled at her and she made a tight smile in reply.

"Thank you," he said.

"There's nothing to thank me for."

"Thank you all the same."

He brushed her cheek with his fingertips and she marvelled at their spider touch, such delicate electricity from such thick fingers. She peered a little closer at his skin.

This world was cruel. Sometimes they would not hold until Carving Mars. Sometimes they would only hold until she fell in love.

They sat in silence for a while, staring at the castle and the rubicund sun sinking behind it. The crenellations of the building fanned out, alternating bands of shrinking light and broadening shadow, until only night remained.

Margaret tried to count the Capital stars, but could only find sixteen.

She glanced at her watch. It was a little too early. She possessed such a poor concept of time.

* * *

The tent unfolded itself quickly, quite a sophisticated model.

Inside, the bed unfurled and grew fat and a hundred small machines clicked on. Margaret did not really believe in roughing it.

Darwin dragged the cooking gear through the door, as she secured the Myartruck, and released half a dozen perimeter flies.

She blinked and one by one their eyes came on. Three hovered by the castle, two above it, another on the ridge. Stag-rabbit males fought on the plain; a female watched with feigned indifference.

Margaret could hear them from where she stood. There was nothing else about but raceroaches and a distant *tonnerrecrane*.

She often wondered what T-zone they came from, if their now was this now.

It wasn't really about time, but memory. They seemed stable enough. What haunted them?

She walked inside and Darwin smiled at her.

She kissed him, then kissed him again: hard.

"Dinner's almost ready," he protested, but not too loudly.

"It can wait."

It did.

* * *

Margaret's eyes snapped open.

Her elegances were jumpy. A couple of alarms were ringing in her head.

Tents, even armoured ones, always made her feel claustrophobic, and vulnerable.

She could hear a storm of *tonnerrecranes* crack-booming across the plain, crashing northwards to where the desert sometimes ended and the grasslands began: depending when she was.

Something else had woken her. One of her perimeter flies was down.

She ran the fly's last images back; caught a brief flickering of movement at the end of the transmission. Slowed a dozen times, it looked like a hand.

She shivered.

Fifteen seconds since that last blurred relay. Margaret peered down at Darwin.

Hard as it was to believe, in sleep his face was even more inno-cent. She decided not to wake him.

Margaret could handle things on her own. She armed. Her body tingled, all her elegances alert. A few of her monitors went red. She whispered them to subliminal, silently commanded the door to open, and rolled outside.

A hand grabbed her, smothering her mouth.

She bit down, hard, and struck out with elbows.

Her assailant fell and two of her perimeter flies, bitter at the loss of a comrade and released by her momentary lapse of concentration, rushed in to blind with bursts of red light.

Margaret's eyes widened when she saw who it was.

"You," she said, and called the flies off. They buzzed angrily around her head before resuming guard.

"Sorry, honey," Alex said. "I'm not sure when I am."

She reached down to help him up, wondering how she was going to explain this to Darwin. Alex's hand gripped hers then crumbled away.

At the loss of weight, Margaret fell flat on her back.

"A Memory. A damn memory," she said, eyes shiny with tears and premonitions. "Oh fuck."

But she wasn't surprised. This whole world was charged with memories. Every damn flake of dust of it, dust that danced and stuck to her, before slipping away again.

She looked North where the *tonnercranes* flew and saw nothing.

Even the stars seemed to have fled the sky.

And all she had left were the ruins of the castle and the dust that all memories here became.

* * *

.

Darwin tapped a self-lighting cigarette to flame a neat, signifi-cant motion, and Margaret watched him revel in the air of sophistication he seemed to think it gave him. The landscape rolled by; each mile a virtual clone of the one behind and the one ahead.

They'd made the straight section of the Run, no curve for more than five hundred miles. The Pilanally Mountains smudged the Western Horizon, running almost parallel with the road. They met up, road and range some eight hundred miles south. And where they met was Carving Mars.

"If you're going to smoke at least open a window."

Darwin laughed and rolled the window down, she watched him for a moment, thinking back—or was it forward?

Margaret had found him in the Glass City, during one of its rests from perambulation, the engines still, the air relatively clear. Correction: he found her, they always did; this time at the Reeker bar. They fell in love that very night on Solemn Peak Ezy as silver moths beat glittering storms around the air vents.

He had been going to rob her but could not bring himself to do it. Such a lousy thief: stole her heart instead.

* * *

The first Starsteamer, trailing fire and fists of smoke, tumbled past early in the afternoon. Its passage rattled the windows of the Myartruck like a palsied ghost. It struck the landing zone a few moments later, shaking the dead bones of this world.

An hour afterwards, another starsteamer pricked the skin of the sky.

Darwin stuck his head out of the window and watched the ship plummet and fume, great engines straining against their fall.

"I'd forgotten that sound. The machinery of the Glass City has nothing on that."

"It's even worse on the inside," Margaret said, remembering that thought-drowning roar. Perhaps it had been designed that way, to deaden the mind, to make bearable what true conscious-ness could not—the massive rumblings of what had been her steel womb. Ten years packed insidem as space and time were distorted, the steamship punching holes through the warp and weft of the universe; turbines shuddering. "It seemed an endless death, I cannot even begin to tell you the pains, the torments of those light years and then, and then the ship was still. Silence but for the great shiftings and tockings of cooling metal."

When the walls came down, the first thing she saw was Carving Mars. But only for a moment before the storm that raced in to hide it.

Darwin gripped her hand. "Nearly there."

"Yes," she said, pushing his hand away and swiping at her eye to catch a tear, or wipe away a grain of dust.

The ground shook as heat and smoke lipped the horizon.

* * *

The market ground was closing as they arrived; Margaret was relieved to find it there at all, even if it was being unmade melting away with the day. Tired men, smoking cigarettes, pulled down their stalls; rolled tight their banners against evening and the ever-present threat of storm.

A few ghotelem performed their cyclical madness, moans and murders and temporo-spatial puppetry, drawing crowds of wide-eyed children. But even the ghost telemetrics would be shutting down soon and the children going home to bad dreams.

"We'll find somewhere to stay. No point doing anything else this evening," Margaret said.

Darwin was excited; he looked this way and that for familiar faces.

"My brother ran a stall. Sold contractware, a penny a piece," he said distractedly. "Before they banned the old money, and the market fell away." He laughed. "I don't suppose he's here."

Margaret looked around. "I don't think so. It would be unlikely, but . . ."

"I'm tired." said Darwin.

"So am I," she said.

* * *

That night she awoke to clamour. A riot of noise coming from outside; the trumpeting of instruments; the bellowing of livestock; the softer reedy cry of flutes.

Darwin was rediscovering innocence in his dreams; she left him there, rolled smoothly and silently out of the bed.

A ghotelem stood in the corner of the room, seemingly unaware of them. It carried out a conversation with the past, kept flickering in and out as though its signal was somehow windblown, scattering and reforming. Hazy eyes stared in her direction but did not see. She hated the things, these domestic haunts, but they were almost impossible to get rid of and harmless. Shrugging, she turned from it and to the noise echoing from the street.

The bedroom had a thick glass sliding door that opened onto a concrete balcony, an odd light washed through—yellow and urgent. She slid the door open—activating the door's noise suppressors so as not to disturb Darwin—then shut it behind her.

A great Sulphur-Sphere floated down the street at the head of a procession—the pseudo sun broke up the night in fits and spits and starts. Men and women, on stilts of gleaming glass, strode behind it, prodding the sphere with cinder-sticks, driving it on at a marching pace. Margaret stared down at them, familiar faces all, chiaroscuro sketches in the jaundiced brilliance. One man waved and winked, a woman blew a kiss. Following the sun-prodders, on the broad backs of mechanical mammoths the size of her Myartruck, rode flautists, violinists and percussionists beating out old Starkin marches with a hint of Sommersetian jiggery.

Ribbons fluttered from the musician's beards and wrists and trailed from their hair. Behind them people danced and sang and poets quoted the Male/Female Ifs.

Every one of them she'd taken here. Every one of them she had loved and lost. Every eye was upon her. She felt pinned and suspended by their gaze.

Above a starsteamer burst the bubble of the atmosphere and streaked low and hard across the sky. Moments later the whole earth shook, the night parade stopped.

As one they bowed and then, dust blew across the street—swirled and undid—darkness behind it, and they were gone.

Darwin awoke at the first contact of her fingers, his eyes dull and startled.

"What time is it?"

Margaret stifled a laugh, she didn't have a clue what T-zone this was. "Just kiss me," she said. "Just kiss me now."

And he did and more.

*　*　*

The next morning Margaret and Darwin wandered the markets. She loved them, these stalls to snare the unwary, the tourist and lander alike.

Carving Mars had been here since the beginning.Here there would be/had been the first dust mines. Here the Diviners would uncover their bright visions. One day. One T-zone. Here the dust was thick, everything veiled in an odd kind of nostalgia.

Jewellery hung in glittering aciniform rows, ripe for the picking. Cheap novel-cards and security flies were available. Things fried and boiled lubricously beneath the eye-burn blue of the sky.

Their stomachs rumbled.

They bought salad rolls, crisp and moist against the soft

dryness of this town and drove up to the Widesphynx. Because that is what lovers do.

"It's beautiful," Darwin said as they stood beneath the stone-beast's massive paws. "And we'll never know who or what built it."

The Widesphynx was carved out of a mountain, its eyes stared West to the landing ground, watching the starsteamers fall, bemusement fixed upon its face.

"A genuine alien artefact," Margaret said and kissed him full upon the lips. Darwin's face was tight with disappointment as he looked down upon the town.

"My past has gone. It's all unravelled."

Margaret brushed his cheek.

"I know. It's what the past does."

Darwin smiled and gripped her hand.

"I shouldn't have expected anything else." He tapped his head. "That's where it all is. In here, I should have left it there."

"It's still there," Margaret said. "It always will be."

Darwin nodded.

"Yes," he said.

A starsteamer fell through the sky. The earth shuddered with its contact, the Widesphynx seemed to nod its head. Margaret followed its lithic gaze.

"Well, only one more place to go and this tour is done." She smiled though her mouth was dry and cold. They ate their salad rolls in silence and stared down at Carving Mars.

* * *

A dust storm came up while they drove down the mountain, forcing them to a crawl as clouds gritty and red swam and shivered against the windscreen.

Margaret sent out flies and followed their signals, slowly, slowly down, a knot of tension building in her neck. Darwin kept quiet, after she snapped at one of his suggestions. They drove in silence, except for the occasional curse thrown by Margaret at the obfuscations of the storm.

At last they reached the valley. A half hour trip grown to nearly two, and, as is often the case with such things, the storm fell away. In moments, it was almost as though it had never happened, but for the grit that coated the windows and the soft leaking of dust through ancient rubber seals.

They drove onto the plain and Carving Mars was gone.

No sign of road or structure. Simple flat and rusty land, virginal and unchartered, as though the town had never been.

As it should have been. As it was and would be for a while.

Darwin's eyes rolled in the back of his head. He shook a little. Margaret reached out a hand to steady him and he pushed it away. Her fingers came back gritty. She brought the sand to her lips and almost cried.

"There isn't much time," he said.

"I know," she replied, struck as she was always struck by their sudden wisdom.

Another starsteamer began its plummet and they followed its smoking tail.

Drove hard.

* * *

The Myartruck was shuddering when Margaret finally brought it to a halt. The glass windshield and the driver's side rear vision mirror were already dipping, dripping dust. The seat beneath her grew insubstantial.

Margaret helped Darwin get out of the vehicle. He let her, eyes wide at what lay before them. Even now, Margaret couldn't help but be impressed.

It was field of the dead: a fallen star field. The massive hulks of starsteamers, shattered by impact, spread all over the plain.

Margaret remembered waking here. She remembered her death. She remembered Carving Mars in the not too distance, where there should have been nothing, where there often was.

Death is itself but a transition.

The ships pulled themselves apart, transformed into hundreds and thousands of machines. Some dove into and dug deep beneath the earth, drawing energy from the still formidable heat of the planet's core, others spread gossamer wings or blew great helium bubbles and drew themselves into the sky.

"Nothing remains. Nothing is wasted. They undo themselves to make a world," Margaret said.

Darwin moaned, his lips cracked. "They make my world, don't they?"

Margaret smiled.

"Yes. At least I think they do."

Margaret shivered, and extended her hands out towards the flowering machinery.

"This world holds memories, Darwin. The dust, it is kind of like time itself. Time grown erratic and doddering or puerile and unwary of things like causality. It picks up moments, events, people, and places and plays them over and over again.

"Do you remember why I drove you here?"

"I wanted to go home."

"Yes, Darwin, yes, that and because maybe I have to take everyone here eventually.

"Perhaps that is my true function. To bring you to this place, one by one, this plain beyond Carving Mars. The dust is everything, without beginning or end, perhaps I am merely its most durable creation."

"But it must begin somewhere. The dust was here. We came here, or will come here."

"Have we? Will we, or is the dust merely fastening upon a possibility, the chance that all this might happen?"

"And out of the spent and unconsidered Earth, the Cities rise again."

"What?" Margaret said blankly, remembering once, when The Glass City had fallen about her, turned to dust. She'd wandered, bound and bewildered by that storm for five days.

Darwin laughed.

"Kipling, it's Kipling."

"Oh, Darwin," she said. "How I hate that I endure. You will never know what that is like. You will never remember."

Then she was gone.

Margaret, a pile of dust.

Darwin reached down and ran it through his fingers.

"Oh, I understand," he whispered, his eyes wet with tears. "I understand because I endure, too. Carving Mars, Mexico, Catacomb City. I will not forget, I promise. Until we meet again."

He climbed to the top of a nearby ridge, sat down and watched the stars come out.

One of them grew larger, filled the sky then fell from it. The ship crashed and cratered the earth with its industry.

And, as it undid itself, he remembered.

COMMUTER

The working day ends.

The air is the temperature of blood; there is no escape from the heat of my body. Homeostasis has made allegiance with the environment. Thinking it somehow to my benefit, my body's mechanics stifle me. Sweat runs down my armpits into the crevices and folds of my flesh, soiling my business shirt in dark uncomfortable ripples.

All of us wait for the train.

There is little conversation. Day's end and heat have drawn the talk from us like a poison. The station's speakers mumble and eruct loudly—distortion and feedback makes the words almost unintelligible.

Something about delays.

As one, we slump into our positions.

I feel the weight of my spine pressing down upon sweat-encased feet. I begin to doubt I'll be able to move when the train comes. I sway a little, try to feel my toes and give up.

The station is deep and a long way from anywhere else.

The tracks ring for minutes before we even hear the train. Tocsins echo and we feel a burst of even hotter air, the flatulence of tunnels, and the demon howl of engines reaches fever pitch.

The train rushes by, crashes by. The Express is filled almost to bursting. Faces pressed against the glass, mouth great Os of dismay.

"Poor bastards," someone says.

Aren't we all?

The train's passage breaks the monotony briefly.

There is a woman standing next to me. She smells of sweat and perfume gone sour. I stare at her neck, and the constellation of pimples there. She feels my gaze and turns. I recognise her dimly. We may have fucked, a long time ago, in some garden of delights. Her body was as warm as this station's heat, warmer perhaps. Her eyes widen, too, and we share a moment of weary contemplation. Those pre-executive days.

Now my cock is rash bound and shrunken and has not stirred from impotence in seventeen years.

There is nothing to talk about.

So we do not.

The train arrives already full. Half a dozen people get off. One of them turns to me.

"How was it?" he asks.

I shrug my shoulders and smile vacuously.

He frowns and trudges towards the escalators. They have broken down; it is a long, slow walk to the top.

I am pushed into the train, and a different kind of heat; the press of human bodies, the fermentation of familiar odours. The air is an acrid miasma of sweat, stale flatulence and bad breath.

We all have bad breath here.

The air conditioners groan and roar to no perceptible effect.

I stand, of course. Those who sit learn to rue the consequences of laziness. You try not to catch their eyes, or stare too long at their endless swallowing, or where flesh and seat have fused.

Three or four stops are all that it takes until they've gone, drowned in the torn fabric of the seats and the smudged buff of red cracked vinyl.

The doors close.

The train pulls from the station, with a lurch that tears something in my locked knees. We enter the tunnel, and darkness crashes down. The train's lights flicker to half-life. The carriages shriek, a dirge of tortured metal, of unoiled hinges and engines only working at fifty-percent efficiency. Through the greasy windows, I see, dimly, obscene graffiti; massive phalluses; distorted vaginas; the sun rising over a field of flowers, mountains distant. I curse at that one.

Someone sobs. Not far from me. It is the woman I recognised at the station.

We lack tolerance—she knows where she is, we all do. We beat the woman into silence. It is an insouciant beating; we take no pleasure from it, though she is senseless by the time we finish. The train stops, in that darkness, and the doors open.

We know the drill. The body is hurled upon the tracks. As the doors shut, I catch a glimpse of dark shapes rushing towards her. I would shudder, but I have seen all this before. I curse the tedium of everyday nightmares.

At last, we come out of the tunnel, into the middle of the city. The grimy windows deepen its sepia tones. The skyscrapers huddle in mute, idiotic bunches. The roads are crammed with traffic, and it does not pay to look too closely at the drivers; theirs is another hell. I have seen the organs splayed upon the dashboard, the compliment of flies, heard the drone of dull and dreadful muzak.

We near the station, and all of us sigh. I am never sure whether we actually utter it, or if it is some mental shuddering we share.

There is an intricate lacework of tracks, branching in and out of the station. I stare at that weave of steel, pathways and possibilities, all of them dreadful.

Terror has no place in hell, just misery.

What grand fears there are seem nothing, what flapping wings, what blood crowned jaw; all these are gotten used to. It is the interminable nature of it all. The endless in and outs. The red tape. The feet that ache from slightly ill-fitting shoes. And this is how they break us. If breaking us is truly their aim, for whatever aims there may have been seem lost. Purpose has fled.

We contemplate it all, every one of us. It bears down, bears down, bears down.

I straighten my tie; the knot rubs against my Adam's apple. I curse and mumble and fiddle with the thing, but it is as comfortable as it gets.

The train comes to a shuddering halt.

I almost trip, and find myself the first at the door. After several jarring tugs at the sticky handle, something comes unstuck and the doors part. I stumble out onto the platform, people jostle past to get inside. The heat hits me—it is the temperature of my heart, the sick humidity of my furred tongue.

Though the city is unfamiliar, I already know where to go.

I look to my watch; I'm running late. A whistle blows. Doors crack shut.

The train slides out behind me.

The working day begins.

ANABIOSIS

I am sitting in a room talking to a dead man. He is smoking a cigarette. What do the dead smoke?

"Whatever we can get," D. Conway says, then grins apologetically. It is a forced grin, like this small talk is forced, but it is all that we are allowed. "These are sixteens, a little too strong for my liking, but what can you do?"

Outside four-hundred-and-thirty-eight dead people live in the cramped confines of Woolamulla holding station. This is the hard end of a miracle.

D. sits there and I can see it in his eyes. He's waiting for the question, the one I have to ask.

"I don't remember. None of us do, and believe me, we've all had time to compare notes.

"I remember dying. Well, I remember the pain and the darkness that followed. Maybe I remember feeling relief, but that could just be me, trying to put some kind of spin on it. But after death and before the AE there was nothing."

But is he happy to be back?

A kind of ambivalence crosses his face. He puts the cigarette down.

"I just don't understand why we're here. We didn't ask for this. We didn't choose to come back from the dead. And we certainly didn't expect to be taken to this place."

The guard—or as they prefer to be called "quality assurers"—cuts our talk short then, and insists on giving me a brief tour of the complex. There are two billiard tables, the felt in one of them ruined, a tennis court and putting green—though with the Drought it is more a putting brown. There is even a pool to the rear of the facility, currently drained though they cannot tell me why.

"It's virtually resort living," the guard says. "Who wouldn't want to stay here?"

When I suggest that that is hardly the point, that these are Australian citizens, and no resorts I have ever been to have razor wire fences or armed guards, his manner changes and I am led from Woolamulla to my car outside.

As I drive away from the complex, I can feel the weight of many envious eyes.

Resort or no, it is still a prison.

RS Magazine, November 200-

* * *

MIRACLE

"Church groups are describing it as a miracle. The scientific community has provided a more low key description, the Anabiotic Event.

On August 27, 200-, the western corner of the Garadan Cemetery came back to life. 433 people, ranging in age from thirteen to ninety eight awoke, naked, above their tombs. In one evening, Garadan's population, on the decrease since the local abattoir closed in 1992, nearly doubled.

"I have never seen anything like it," said Travis Smith, the cemetery caretaker who found them. "At first I thought it was one of those arty things. You know when they take photos of crowds in the nude. But then I saw the mud and the look of shock on their faces. And there wasn't a single camera anywhere that I could see. And I knew. I just knew."

Emergency forces were flown in immediately, though it wasn't until several days had passed that the truth was confirmed.

Courier News, August 27, 200-

* * *

"What we do we know about these people? Very little. Of course, those with immediate family still alive, should be assimilated as quickly as possible. But our records are sketchy for most of the cemetery. How many of them committed crimes in their first lifetime? Shouldn't those who were serving a life sentence be returned to prison? Just because God—or whatever was responsible for the Anabiotic Event—gave these people, in this particular Cemetery, a second chance doesn't mean that our society has to, *if they don't deserve it.*

"The implications of this miracle must be explored before any action is taken."

Liberal Senator Harlan Stapleton—September 4, 200-

* * *

DEAD BREAK OUT OF WOOLAMULLA

Five dead men and two dead boys broke out of Woolamulla Holding Station yesterday. One of them, it has been revealed, is a convicted criminal and is believed to be dangerous.

Daily Star, October 16, 200-

* * *

GAMMA BURSTS MAY HAVE CAUSED DEAD TO RISE

Twin Gamma Ray bursts on the night of what scientists call the Anabiotic Event have led to recent speculation that there may be a link between the two.

Doctor Howsmith of the Missouri Institute is certain both bursters, as they are popularly called, flashed on at the same time. "It's not a matter of coincidence, it's a matter of cause and effect."

Doctor Howsmith's theories have been scoffed at by the Scientific Community, who claim that not only are Gamma Ray Bursters incredibly common, but also believed to have their origin far across the Universe.

"These bursters did not originate at the time of the AE," Professor Willard of MIT explained. "These bursts occurred before the dinosaurs even walked the earth, let alone humans. They're that far away."

Doctor Howsmith's response is simple.

"Once the dead walk amongst us, anything is possible."

Regardless, those twin bursts have now been called "The Eyes of God," a name Professor Willard describes as unfortunate.

Sunday Colour Post—October 200-

* * *

FIVE ESCAPEES DIE AGAIN

In a dramatic shoot out today on the Hume highway, five of the seven escapees were killed while trying to hijack a bus. There were no civilian or police casualties. Reports that the escapees were unarmed have yet to be confirmed or denied by the Federal Police.

According to a source in the Woolamulla camp, conditions are worsening, and in the forty-degree celcius heat, tempers, as well as temperatures, are rising.

Aus- Newspaper October 16 200-

* * *

Get your Eyes of God poster today
Sunday Colour Post—November 200-

* * *

Caller 26: "Look, Alan. They've lived their lives. They should go back where they came from."

AL: "You mean kill them?"

Caller 26: "No, ah, that's not what I'm talking about, though some'd say they're already dead. They should be shipped out. Give them an island somewhere. This is our country and it is a land of the living. What if they all came back, could we accept that?"

AL: "I agree. This is an issue on which we need a strong government."

Alan Laws, Radio Nation, November 10, 200-

* * *

It's so hot today. I think my brains are baking. When we make too much trouble, or just piss off the guards, they shut down the air conditioners. We don't have television or even radio.

We had a television at one stage, but someone got mad, kicked it with their boots till it smashed. After that, we didn't have a television anymore.

Where's mum and dad? I'd only been gone four years, but no one is telling me anything. When I woke up, I thought this was heaven, but it can't be. This is hell. I am sure of it.

All I want is to see my family again.

Why are we here? We didn't choose this.

From the Diary of Nancy Curlew

* * *

RIOTS KILL TWENTY

After what has been descbed as the suicide of fourteen year old Dead Detainee Nancy Curlew, Woolamulla station was the scene of rioting yesterday. Fires are still blazing in the western quarter of the station and at least twenty of the detainees are dead.

The rest are expected to be shifted to a higher security complex.

Both the UN and Amnesty International have condemned the continued detention of the dead.

The Deputy Prime Minister countered their claims today, branding them misinformed and emotional.

"What we are doing is perfectly legal under international law."

Newsline Post, December 11 200-

* * *

THOUSANDS PROTEST TREATMENT OF RESUR-RECTED AUSTRALIANS

Hundreds of thousands of Australians protested today against what organisers claim to be the inhuman conditions in which the dead have been forced to live at Woolamulla Holding Station.

Marcus Owen, head of the protest in Sydney, spoke to the crowd and attendant media.

"Our agenda is quite straight forward. We want them released immediately. These are Australians, they have done nothing wrong."

The Prime Minister appeared unmoved, whilst celebrating people's right to protest, he said it did not reflect popular opinion.

"The majority of Australians support our policy. You must remember, too, that some of these Resurrected Australians were in fact criminals."

Adelaide Post, November 20, 200-

* * *

THE DEAD ZONE.

Kirabirra Holding Station is just five kilometres out of town. Children still ride their bikes to the edge of the ridge, just before the station, hoping to catch a glimpse of the dead. I have spoken to several of them.

What have they seen?

Nothing, just guards.

After the Woolamulla Riots, the dead were shifted out here. For the past two days now, I have been trying to gain access. And failing.

I was warned that this would be the case, nor did I expect to be the exception. No journalist has walked through these doors in ten months.

Most papers seem almost to have forgotten Kirabirra exists. Without riots or information leaks, this story is as moribund as those behind the walls once were.

Kirabirra Holding Station is a no-go zone and the rights of its thousand or so dead a grey area. When you come back from beyond the grave, it seems you are no longer a citizen of Australia. You are no longer a citizen of any nation or bound by any laws but those imposed upon you.

I walk towards the gatehouse and two guards are waiting for me there.

Both are armed with rifles.

I take a photo and the guns are raised.

"We'll have that, thank you."

One of the guards expertly extracts my film.

"This is a quarantined zone. I must insist that you return to your car, sir."

He is polite but implacable, and his gun is pointed at my chest.

I nod, glancing up and discovering that these aren't the only guns aimed at me. Sentries look down from every corner.

Kirabirra appears to have tighter security than a maximum-security prison and, as far as I can tell, it is more to keep people out than in.

Fly overs are illegal. The excuse that this is a terrorist sensitive area, that these people just want to keep their privacy, that in the treatment of the dead the government is just not answerable to the public, none of these things cut it.

There are secrets here.

And we have protested and we have demanded and nothing is done. We grew up in a world where we believed in "people power", that if enough people shouted loudly they would have to listen.

And we discovered that they did not. That protests peter out. That people forget. And secrets grow.

Insiders Magazine Sept 200-

* * *

PICTURES REVEAL FIELD OF DEAD?

Kirabirra Holding Station appears to hold nothing but corpses. Pictures leaked to the public today show the Holding Station filled with what look like unmarked graves.

The Prime Minister, in an address to the Press Club, has denied such claims explaining only that the Kirabirra Holding Station was a cover up, but of a different sort.

"The dead have been reassimilated. This government believes in giving all Australians a fair go. We wanted to provide these people with as normal a life as they could have. And the best way we could do that was in the creation of new identities for each of them. It was, as you may have guessed, a massive undertaking. What these people choose to do with their lives now is up to them, but it is our duty as Australians to let them live out those lives with dignity and anonymity."

Newsnet, September 10 200-

* * *

KIRRABIRRA EMPTY BUT NO GRAVES FOUND

News Link

* * *

NEW WASTE FURNACE ALREADY DRAWING HEAT

The Controversial Pullamin Industrial Waste Incinerator has already drawn criticism. Last week the neighbouring township of Indoorilla complained of an extremely dense pall of smoke emanating from the Furnace.

"It's bad enough most weeks, but I've never seen so much smoke. Thick dark cloud. It started late at night and didn't stop until the next day."

Government officials won't confirm or deny the report, blaming it on odd environmental conditions.

"It was a weird confluence of events. Regardless of the cause, we can just about guarantee it won't happen again," Federal Environment Minister Krowley said yesterday.

Newsline, September 13, 200-

DON'T GOT NO WINGS

's a place I know where the shadows stay long and you get off the bus at a shelter bare lit, so everything looks bloodless and sick, and roofed in curled and rusted sheaths of corrugated iron.

There's an art nouv picture of a very pretty girl, but someone writ the word "fuck" across that lovely, lonely girl's face and "titties" across her breasts.

's still beautiful, regardless of such wit, and some comfort, 'cause I get off me bus there most days, makes me laugh sometimes, sometimes it makes me cry.

I sit on the bus waiting for that stop, waiting for that picture and I never know how I'm going to feel. Funny. I can have the best day and it will end in tears, or I can have the worst and it will end in tears or laughter.

"How you feelin' today?" Driver asks me, just about every time, unless he's sick and it's someone else.

"I don't know," I says, every time, unless he doesn't ask me because he's not there. "But you can watch me, in that rear view, once I'm done with the day and started with the feeling."

"I'll be watching," he says or doesn't.

I get off and the bus drives away and I look at that pretty picture and I feel. I look past the words and I feel.

Cicadas are singing in the awful heat and the roof's singing too, creaking and shifting to the last caresses of the sun, and the wind that chases it, and I look away from that picture and back at the city where I endured 'nother nine to five.

City's a slag heap, bottomless, monstrous and vile. City's a slag heap and I made it through another day.

"Fly with me," my picture says and I whistle sad.

"Don't got no wings," I say.

"Fly with me."

"Don't got no wings."

And I'm sad that day and the girl is sad and the bus is out of sight and I get on my way home, out here where most of the houses are gone, or ruined stubs of residences, like a suburb what forgot to clean its teeth most nights, so everything went rotten.

always clean my teeth, but some people don't.

make my tea. And sit alone, on the good bit of my verandah and stare at that carcass of a suburb. My back is sore from all that factory work. I've got my favourite book. I got it again. I buy one copy whenever I find it, so I can have it, whenever I want it. That cat sure made a mess, but the kids liked him, 'cause he cleaned up afterwards and their parents were happy. I remember when death came and things went septic, the whole suburb went infected. Not many didn't die, but I didn't.

I tried to clean up afterwards, but there was too much mess.

The moon's full.

I sit and watch the moon and the ships come launched out of the belly of the city in the East. Flame and fury into the sky.

I work there, but I don't got no wings.

I watch until my eyes start to flutter, heavy with the coming sleep, and I make my careful way across the rotting, yawning floorboards into my room.

The house shakes and another ship challenges the light of the moon.

* * *

Something wakes me.

Something that's not a ship breaking the sky.

There's voices and laughter, coming from outside, and I get out of bed and venture outside. Outside, it's hot and the moon is still huge in the sky.

They're knocking down my bus shelter.

I run and they see me and suddenly there's guns aimed and I think I'm going to die, but I don't stop 'cause death is less scary.

"We're building you a new bus shelter," the Driver says.

"But you don't have to," I say.

The Driver shakes his head, looks at me like I'm stupid, dismisses me.

"Of course, we have to."

They start on the picture. Tearing it down. My picture, perfect ruined picture. And I beg and they say, "Go away, we've work to be doin'. Go away."

I cry, like tears, and I run and they beat me with their guns until the driver says, all worried.

"Don't hurt him, lads. Don't hurt him."

But the hurt is done and I find that darkness runs ragged and sticky in my skull, sticking to my thoughts, swallowing, swallowing, and I want to fly, but I don't got no wings.

* * *

I wake all sick and sore and would call in sick, but they don't like that, so I get out of bed. The Driver put me back here, or maybe it was a dream. A dream. I run to the veranda and see it there.

And it's the awful wonder of the new.

A new bus shelter waits, and the city waits behind it. Only

the city ain't new, it's the same old slag, just lit up with the sun, just waiting.

I would call in sick, but they don't like that.

* * *

"How you feelin' today?" Driver asks me. Work done, just the trip home.

And I don't answer.

"How you feelin' today?" Driver asks me, again.

And I don't answer, again, so he stays quiet, maybe looks guilty, 'cause of my bruises.

"I'll be watching," he says, quiet, maybe so I wouldn't hear, but I do as I get off the bus. Into that empty shelter, smelling cement and new shadows and feeling the winds coming up, chasing the sun.

Then I see a bit of the picture, just a corner, and I reach for it, but the hot wind lifts it, lifts it, lifts it, into the air.

Lifts it high and West, into the air, until the sun blinds, so that even my eyes can't follow.

I want to follow, to chase that picture bit, to chase the winds that chase the sun, but I can't follow, 'cause I don't got no wings.

PORCELAIN SALLI

Alarm bells rang.

Common enough in a state of Anthozoan war. Tocsins echoing: warning of collisions imminent or induline spore clouds and polyps drifting and falling like death.

But this clamour was different, urgent and strange.

Porcelain Salli blinked and eased her focus from the SOL-Stream, shaking off the thoughts clinging to her—tenacious and earthly fog tendrils slow to lift.

Her brains were next-to-full-up, and her reserves stung—migraines waiting to happen, in skull's fore and aft, if she wasn't careful.

Time to purge.

Bemused, though, she found it hard to cull the SOL-Stream stuff. For once Jupiter's magnetosphere wasn't acting up and the signal coming through was clean and fat and she felt alive to all its possibilities.

Jet spiders and whispers, squirts of almost infinitely dense information, the by-product of the Simpson Sentiences; the thoughtshit on which the rest of the Solar System fed.

She'd glimpsed on the periphery, where meaning and noise warped, becoming convoluted webs of possibility, a dozen Dorothies, all of them blinking and slapping their ruby slippers together, like they were getting off on getting out.

Salli blinked again and a polyp tentacular mass reached over from its cup, brushing her porcelain face lovingly, but insistently, pulling her completely out of the virtual and into the visceral.

Salli blinked again.

"Anty M?"

The sirens increased in pitch, becoming a constant and terrible shriek.

Anty M whispered once. Part scent, part sonics.

HOLD ON.

Tentacles, sprung from nearby cups and hollows, bunched around her, gripped her waspish waist and squeezed, gentle but strong.

The world swung upside down.

Everything shuddered, coral alleys twisted, bits of the ceiling collapsed in clouds of calcium carbonate, and, deep below, terabytes worth of bio-processors went out and reserves came online.

Anty M held its Salli tight, for it had raised her, grew her. Losing Salli would be a kind of death.

Then the world was done shaking, the sirens ran down, and Anty M loosened its hold, though the tentacles remained, worried and stroking.

"What was that?" Salli asked, then purged and listened.

* * *

"A ship," she said.

"A shuttle," Anty M corrected. "A ship that goes between ships."

The shuttle teetered before her, bulbous metal all twisted, crumpled and broken: gases streamed from a dense network of cracks along its diamond hull, freezing and icicle-jetting off into the frigid dark.

Anthozoan flesh had cracked and cratered beneath its impact, but Anty M had held together, which was more than could be said for the shuttle. As Salli watched, one of the mangled landing claws gripping the hard surface of the Anthozoan, gave way silently and the shuttle plunged forward. Anty M's nearest tentacles whipped back into their cups, then all was still. But for the red spot behind, shifting, shifting, fluid and vast.

Salli's eyes possessed elegances set to detect the biological and they did just that.

Something, that wasn't an Anthozoan spore, lived inside.

Barely.

She was watching it die.

"Can I?" She asked. "Can I save it?"

Anty M could deny its Salli nothing.

She linked with the wreck's dry mind. Easy enough, as the shuttle's networks were bleating and sad.

On contact, Salli paused, shocked at what she found, the AI possessed very different thoughts to that of Coral; corridors of desiccated sentience that did not curl and pucker. At first it denied her, but when it realised that Salli was not going away, and that she might just save its occupant, it gave a brittle sigh and released the shuttle's doorifice.

A last gasp of atmosphere escaped, a frosty exhalation that left Salli wiping ice from her eyes. And when she had, they SOL-Webd.

"Oh my," she whispered into the soundless vacuum. "A man."

And indeed it was.

A ruined man, skin blistered with sealant and webbing that could not hide the facts. The cockpit window was an impasto of frozen blood. His limbs were twisted and his bones fractured. Ribs, gone rogue, had punctured a lung.

And that was the least of it.

A man broken and dying. But not dead yet.

She lifted him up and carried him inside, where Anty M was already filling a chamber with air.

* * *

Dava Grey, the shuttle's AI had called him, and the name was sown into his suit in a glittery but bloodstained thread. In the oxygenated chamber, she looked closely but fleetingly over her patient. Sealant kept the blood in, but could do nothing about the deeper damages, impact woundings, boiling haemorrhages, blood vessels undammed. She had no knowledge of such things, but she knew where she could find it.

Into the SOL-Web she plunged, thankful the signal was strong, hunting and gathering all things pertinent and medical. Cavitation. Tension Pneumothorax. Hemothorax. Cardiac Tamponade. A minute, no more and she knew what to do, what she had to make.

Along coral alleys and down twisted staircases she ran to the Sound Box at the heart of the coral. Here was true weightlessness, no down to warp its makings, she programmed in her needs with urgent stabs of her fingers, marvelling all the while at the magic of acoustic manufacture, baffles and lasers and frequencies shifting and shaping the raw matter funnelled into the chamber.

Here she had been constructed, and her occasional emergency repairs effected. With the chamber you could make just about anything, if you possessed the right template. But after Salli had been made Anty M rarely used it, materials were scarce and better used in extending the colony.

When the tools were finished—cutters, rebuilders and the

like, down to needles for injecting and tubes for sucking, nano and macro medicines—she raced back to her Dava Grey patient and cut and dosed.

With the subtleties of soundspun craft, she plucked him from Death's unsubtle grip.

* * *

Sometimes when she was up surface—Anty M's external tentacles waving around her, a forest of hunger—doing her job, breaking free the predatory polyps budded and drifted over from rival colonies, Porcelain Salli would pause and stare at the vast storm-banded gas giant which dominated the heavens.

Tired of chores, lonely and maudlin, she would dream of other places.

That Great Red Spot, where might it take her?

An anticyclone the size of worlds! Dorothy, eat your heart out.

Salli would stare until her eyes iced over or Anty M nudged her, directed her to another front in this slow and endless campaign. All Salli had ever known was war and the quiet spaces between invasions that might stretch a month or a year, filled with the static-haunted susurration of the SOL-Web.

Once a year, Anty M would spawn, light up and crackle with deeply stored energies, ejecting its spore into the cold. Most were devoured by gobbling old Jove, but some of the millions, launched like multi-coloured rain in reverse, maybe just four or five, would collide with a small lump of rock or ice or dead coral and grow.

And perhaps one might even find a more established Anthozoan colony, attach itself to the surface and chew and bud and chew, transmitting to its sister spores, drawing more and more in, until the host colony was consumed and transformed.

Anty M was proud of its Spartoi. Humans were rare—even vacuum-resistant Spartoi—in this radiation filled space between Jupiter and Mars. Dexterous fingers attached to dexterous minds.

It could not begin to conceive of itself as a cold and lonely place for porcelain girls loved and grown by coral.

* * *

At last, Dava Grey rose above the chaos of his pained dreaming and the memory of Death's now distant kingdom. He opened his eyes and looked upon his saviour.

Such a pretty face and he was in love from that moment, till his last.

It was easy to fall in love when you have lost it all. It was easy to fall in love in the cold and the dark, last memories of collision, of sirens screaming, and a big mass looming like death. His patched heart quivered, his pupils dilated.

"You look like—"

"Miss Garland, I know," she said "Dorothy, though my name is Porcelain Salli. Porcelain Salli, Spartoi."

"A good omen. A good omen indeed. Looking like Dorothy, I mean," he said.

And Dava Grey, brave and lost, cried.

* * *

After the crying was done, and Salli brushed at his face gently, gently, and patted and whispered and said nice things, Dava Grey tried to stand. And blacked out.

Anty M was rather amused. Humans were such frail things.

* * *

Salli looked down at her human and waited for his eyes to open again. With the blood gone from his face and the bruising diminishing to shadows he was beautiful. And his voice. Oh his voice! It was honey in her ears.

When Dava Grey stirred, again, she pressed her hand gently but firmly against his shoulders.

"You're still a long way off standing, I'm afraid. Just concentrate on healing, there are bones to knit and wounds to seal up. A few days, no more, and you'll be perfect."

"Where am I?" he asked.

"Home," Salli said. "Coral Sentience Anthozoa Y@M. Anty M for short."

Dava Grey nodded.

"I have heard of the Anthozoans, and their war, but never expected to encounter a colony." He shook his head. "I have no home, mine is long lost. I am at your service, my lady."

* * *

And he had stories to tell. There was a lot the SOL-Web had not told her. But then it was a whisper, a continual babble.

So, she knew nothing of the distant seed-ship-city-mind, *Slow*, stalled on the edge of the Solar System. Or that there, on the edge, was where humankind stopped.

"We embarrass them, see. Our Terran AIs are too ashamed of their parents to let them out and play. No diaspora for the dim-witted fleshlings.

"But Simpson Sentiences are not as clever as they think." Dava Grey puffed up, then hunched down, a long finger pushed against his lips as he whispered, "We travel in silence, exploring, broadening our knowledge. Getting nowhere fast, because speed makes waves, and they would catch us and send us back. I dare not try to chase her, my ship, lest my noisy engines chop up the still black waters and give away the game."

He told her about his ship, *The Melancholy Fled*, its cramped confines, the crowd and smell of crew. Eighty-nine in all, though they had lost nearly a dozen in their slow progress across the solar system. The ship's sails billowed clever and transparent, for such a vast opaqueness would have surely given them away. But bad things happened regardless of cleverness, collisions, bursts of radiation in unguarded moments. People die.

"Earth and Mars where the womb-born live. That is where we both come from—conceptually, you and I—though neither of us was made there. My parents, and those of my crew, were born on a habitat in a small hollowed-out planetesimal. However, it was the AI of *The Melancholy Fled* that raised us. Our parents had to hide us as rubbish and launch us into space and only there, once we were away from the home rock, in the less guarded void, could we grow.

"I have recordings, though, of mother and father. I've seen the small forest of our habitat; I've sampled the odours of that different place. But on Earth, as there is on Mars, there are mighty forests, and on the moon they have trees as large as forests and a great big sack of atmosphere."

"Are they ever lonely?"

"Never and always."

Anty M buzzed for her then. Salli grimaced, but none-the-less she clambered surface-wise to unpick another hungry bit of foreign coral. And while she was gone, Anty M's inner eyes stared at this Dava Grey. And its deeper darker bio-circuitry burned with Anthozoan jealousies.

But Salli adored him and Anty M adored her, so it just watched and Dava Grey healed.

* * *

What times they had.

Talk, not just chatter-flood of the SOL-Stream, or the

chiming deliquescent demands of Anty M, but true interactiveness.

He spoke of the vastness of space, of the other oceanic analogues he'd seen. Great Sentient Sponges on the inner asteroids. A shivering school of proton-hungry squid that shaped itself into a glittering sphere at the approach of *The Melancholy Fled*, then disappeared with an inky squirt of FTL.

And, more recently, Europa, teeming with life beneath the thick, thick ice. But what sort of life was uncertain, they had been unable to get close enough to look. Dava Grey had tried taking the shuttle out for recon, and ended up here, he said, encountering a different sort of life altogether.

The Solar System, let alone the universe, was vast and cold and dead—until you looked a little closer and saw all the things teeming there, clinging to the shadows.

Humans had engineered most of them.

The Anthozoans, for instance. Coral worlds to house humans on interstellar journeys and to seed the great interstices of space with slow-building way stations. But then the Simpson Sentiences had locked down the Solar System.

Where once Anthozoans were destined for the expanses of the galaxy, now they were crowded around Jupiter, possessed of a the desire to spawn and a rudimentary propulsion system too weak to do much beyond stabilising their orbits and avoiding collisions. No wonder they were at war.

All of this was fascinating to Salli and inspirational.

"Perhaps we could build a ship."

Salli stroked his cheek and crooned.

"Think of it! Jaunts to Callisto and Europa, we could take a dip beneath her icy petticoats. No need for either of us to be trapped."

Dava Grey's eyes brightened and Salli said what she'd dared not hope a few weeks before.

"There are rainbows out there somewhere and we might get over them."

Dava Grey laughed and it was a grim sound, for he had seen the face of death and he had spent his life in hiding, running, crouching, looking for shadows.

"There are no rainbows, my love. Just cruel promises and the cold of space. So cold and yet it calls us, hooks in our bones and pulls."

* * *

Dava Grey came up surface with her, wrapped in a thick suit, thicker still with Simpson Sentience technology—a Van Allen belt around his waist and Elegant eyes alert to enemy activity.

He looked at his shuttle and shuddered. The metal that had twisted crazily, the blood-splattered cockpit. Something buzzed a moment in his head. And he thought of the impact again and his plans gone utterly awry.

He gripped Salli's hand. There were always complications.

Salli stared at the wreck admiringly.

"Anty M says I can keep it. A kind of monument to you."

Dava Grey nodded and unlocked the doorifice. It irised open begrudgingly. He reached in and plucked out a few items. One, a small nugget of bone or stone, he looked at wryly, made to throw away then thought better of it, slipping it into his suit pocket.

"What is that?" Salli asked of him.

Dava Grey shrugged.

"A memento. A reminder."

There was a bright flash in the corner of his vision. He pointed, grabbing Salli's hand to help her sight along. "Look, a mining craft skimming Jupiter like a stone!"

The hydrogen-hungry ship shot brilliant as a star out of Jupiter's atmosphere.

His Elegant eyes—enhanced for distance and recognition—mapped out all the major happenings in the Jovian system. Jupiter's Galilean satellites, Europa gleaming like a billiard ball, Angry Io and fat Ganymede and Callisto where the wild things were.

"Yes," he said. "A ship would be fine."

* * *

They hacked into Dava Grey's old computer, digging out its blueprints, and programmed and refined, building a ship for two.

The Ruby Slipper, made of diamond, of course, spun diamond with a crust of delicate red. A pocket ship to be constructed in the Acoustic Chamber then shaken out on the surface.

When not working on *The Ruby Slipper* they slept in Dava Grey's air-filled coral alley, whispering and dreaming, and Salli would stir and look down at her love realising that she did not feel lonely, had not felt lonely since the day the sirens rang.

And all the while, Anty M watched, a thousand eyes and ears all attuned to Salli's laughter, Salli's happiness that was Anty M's not at all.

* * *

"Where shall we go?" Salli asked with *The Ruby Slipper* nearly done. All they needed was to take it up surface and shake it out.

Dava Grey was thoughtful.

"Not far at first, maybe a little hop to Io. We don't want to draw any attention."

"Are there people there?"

"Once, vulcanologists, two whole clans of them. But that was centuries ago. People don't get to go where they want to any more."

A siren rang a familiar bleeping, and Salli smiled wearily.

"I'll be back soon," she said.

* * *

Tentacles closed around him and the air filled with a stinging garrulous odour.

DAVA GREY. Anty M said, startling him, as he'd never heard the Coral Sentience speak. DAVA GREY YOU ARE TAKING AWAY MY SALLI. The voice was a wet one, a threatening babble. DAVA GREY, I WON'T LET YOU.

Anty M's tentacles gripped with obdurate rage.

Dava Grey struggled, but could not pry himself free. Instead, he reached into his pocket and pulled out the stone he had taken from his ruined craft.

"I love her," he said.

I MADE HER.

FED HER.

GREW HER.

THERE IS ONLY ENOUGH LOVE FOR ONE. SHE IS MY SOLDIER.

A tentacle flexed and squeezed and Dava Grey felt something burst: a liquid pain washed through his chest.

Anty M was a warrior that had fought in a conflict over eight centuries old. It had survived by not losing.

War makes creatures cruel. Dava Grey understood that better than most.

He smiled, a little blood leaking from his lips.

"Well, you have lost this time," he said, and opened his fist, whispering a single word. A pass word, a Anthozoan word.

The stone hovered beneath his open palm then shot towards a coral wall.

* * *

Anty M recognised it at once.

CNIDOCYTE! It hissed, flicking at the vileness with a

tentacle and missing. It was a little viral thing that would eat Anty M from the inside out.

Dexterous hands. Dexterous minds.

The cnidocyte struck the far end of the chamber, then flexed: a barbed nematocyst, a thread laden with enemy DNA, punctured the wall.

Anty M shook Dava Grey, hard.

LIES.

LIES.

YOU ARE ALL LIES, MAN.

"Yes," Dava Grey said, colours dancing before his eyes. "Yes and no. My ship encountered another Coral Sentience, in fact, a whole Coral Collective—seems you've got them running scared—and made a deal. For certain heat shield technologies and the Sound box stuff as well, if we could do this for it. Of course I never intended to crash my shuttle. I gave up my chance of escape so that *The Melancholy Fled* could truly live up to its name."

His grin grew wider and bloodier. Death's face loomed but he'd already seen it before. It had lost its terror for him.

"And you know I nearly didn't do it, because I loved her. And because she loved you. But I had promises to keep, Anthozoa Y@M. Promises to keep. If Salli wasn't so good, the other Coral wouldn't be gunning for you. Be proud of that. My Salli, your Salli. She's her own Salli now."

"I'm sorry, truly sorry," Dava Grey said as the Anthozoan shuddered.

Anty M squeezed again, tighter than before and organs ruptured and bled.

Dava Grey's grin turned idiotic, his tongue bloated, and his eyes seemed almost to pop out of his head.

TOO LATE, Anty M thought.

TOO LATE.

Already the virus was spreading, devouring, and when the

cruel enemy DNA reached its core it would send out signals and Anty M's bleached dead bulk would drown in enemy polyps.

SALLI. It called.

Just once, but it was enough.

* * *

Salli lay Dava down, and cried the chalky things that passed for her tears.

Her kisses were dry and hard, and he did not feel them. The same matter of a few minutes before—all sensation—was now insensate.

She stroked his lifeless cheeks and closed the unfluttering eyes of her love.

And for all that, it stung Anty M that she'd not come to it first, it whispered, sadly.

SALLI CHILD.

SALLI CHILD. I AM DYING.

DAVA GREY, HE VIRUSED ME, A CNIDOCYTE.

BUT THEN I AM NO BETTER. I DIDN'T WANT TO LOSE YOU. NOW EVERYTHING IS LOST. I'M SORRY.

DO WHAT YOU MUST, MY LOVE. GO.

"I can't," she said. "I won't."

YOU MUST.

WHAT IS COMING IS NOT CALM, BUT CHAOS.

IT WILL KILL YOU.

Tentacles brushed her back. Sad and stern scents filled the corridors.

GO, GO.

IF YOU LOVED US, GO.

So Salli stumbled to the acoustic chamber. The pocket ship sat there, she picked it up and pulled herself surface-wise. And even as she did, the coral alleys gave up their last—tentacles spilled senselessly from their cups—and all Anthozoan Frequencies grew shrill with viral broadcasts.

HERE, HERE DEVOUR.

* * *

Already polyps were falling, striking the coral, digging and devouring. Drawn by that noisy cnidocyte.

Up surface, Anty M's tentacles shuddered mindlessly or floated limp. Salli paused a moment, missing their conscious touch. Jupiter filled the sky and the polyps kept falling.

Salli found a clear space and flicked her wrists. *The Ruby Slipper* unfolded smoothly, then clicked and expanded.

What a perfect little ship!

The Ruby Slipper glowed, a teardrop of blood.

Salli rubbed the doorifice until it irised open.

The Ship's AI was simple, and downloaded itself into Salli before the doorifice had shut.

"Good," she said. "Good, this is not at all hard."

The hard part was done. The hard part was past. And it hurt her more than she could have ever feared.

The little ship lifted off and Salli turned her back on Jupiter and the almighty storm it contained.

The galaxy itself was a twister eight hundred thousand light years across.

What a storm. What a storm!

No tinpot Kansas cyclone.

The Ruby Slipper shivered, as though in anticipation, and Salli wondered where it would hurl her? What looming wondrous rainbows she might get over: vast enough to make Dorothy envious.

She turned the stealthy engines to full speed, programmed in the coordinates for the most distant star and found out.

PERSUASION

You know this. Of course, you do. But I was there.

For a time, a decade or two, in old Redoubt, words were powerful. The Mechanism behind the world within The Bottle Grande (the vast underlying machinery and all that shifts the substance of that which drifts within the endless sea) became suddenly attentive and talk grew significantly more puissant.

It was not so much that people would believe anything, but that the Mechanism would.

A chaos of unbridled chatter reigned for a moment, but that swiftly gave way to something else. Those that spoke well rose high and fast and he spoke well, my Master, James Collins.

"Eloquence is reality," He said to me, once—when it was literally true—after he had come back early from Parliament; they had whispered a swift close to the day, all those perfectly garrulous folk tired of powerful talk. "And reality is bound by words, the right words, the appropriate ones, and then those words are truth. That is the source of power. Which is why one must always be careful in what one says, or even writes."

"Right you are, Sir," I said, brushing his jacket free of snow and dirt. "Right you are."

He laughed at that, his bright eyes flashing. "Oliver, I am

certain of the air and earth's attentiveness, but do you ever listen to a word I say?"

Then he was gone, striding to his rooms and the solace of good brandy and the meat of his lexicons, leaving me staring down at the wreck and ruin of his costume; wondering why he didn't just talk it all clean and let me get on with some other work. But I knew the truth in that; idle hands are the Devil's whisperings. These busy labours kept my hands busy and my mouth shut.

My Master was wrong; I listened to every word he said. I listened harder than he might care I did, but it is the most important part of my job, without such attentiveness who knows what mischiefs might result.

Twelve years I'd worked for him, almost since boyhood and indenture. I'd cleaned up after him, nodded as he described the heated Debates, the woundings that words can bring even in such a civilised Parliament as ours. He was a good man by any measure, just curse-blessed with power, and the will to use it, of a sort enough to challenge any good. Such are the stresses and strains of the Speakers of Parliament.

I cleaned and polished and set about making fixes and when done, I saw to the evening meal, while he made more mess about the house as was his right.

Even then I had begun to suspect that my Master might be in love.

* * *

And I was right.

Thursday and Rain Day as Parliament decreed it, the down pipes chattering, the roads slick, the parklands thirsty and the distant circuit of the bottle, look up and you can see its curvature, all hazy with downpour.

I accompanied him to the Lady Philpatrick's house on

Worrimer Street, a fashionable place of which the Master had always been disparaging. Three times he poked his head through the carriage window, demanding of the driver why were not yet there and bringing his head back in hair slick and dripping, and whispering it dry.

My Master, the very element of composure had become anything but. I had never known him so red faced, so stilted in his animation or expression.

He had met her quite by accident at a grand dinner hosted by an allied Parliamentarian. A fellow with such meagre persuasive skill that my Master would rarely have anything to do with him, but that day the gentleman had come upon a couple of nearly perfect sentences and my Master, so impressed, had forgotten to not to attend the banquet.

"I was charmed," my Master said. "She charmed me, just with a glance or two I swear. We barely said a word to each other. Is it possible to fall in love from across the room?"

I had no answer for that, so I brushed his hat and wondered what could have transformed my Master so swiftly and ridiculously.

* * *

I understood the moment we entered the drawing room.

Let me say she possessed beauty, but not how you might think it. Hers was a beauty of movement, a beauty of wit and penetrating eyes. You could not love (or even be merely smitten by) wisdom and clarity and joy and not love her.

And my Master held these things to be above all else.

"Mr Collins," she said. "I am delighted to have your company, though somewhat bemused. For I am yet to understand what appeal I might hold to a Member of Parliament."

My Master raised one hand and shook his head. "No, I am the one delighted. Delighted that you agreed to see me."

The Lady smiled at him uneasily, then looked over at me, her eyes weighted with enquiry. I shrugged my shoulders, tried for a reassuring grin, and hoped that this might continue a little better than it had begun.

In that I needn't have worried. The Lady asked all manner of questions concerning the Parliament and the Grammar, and above all that my Master liked to talk about was Grammar.

* * *

"The glorious age of old Redoubt and the world within the Bottle Grande began with the word. And so it has remained," he said to the Lady. "In Parliament we talk and shape. Each sentence is a thunderous proclamation echoing from the bottle's firmament to its distant tapering neck and out of which our society is made."

The Lady raised one eyebrow, and glanced askance at him. "But surely, Mr Collins, there must be a limit to the power of eloquence."

"Other than removing the Bottle Grande itself—for there have been madmen who tried and failed—none that I have encountered," my Master said. "One can talk night into day should one wish it, though a man singularly engaged might take longer than a day or night to do it. Which is why we have the Parliament. A multitude of voices, a choir with which to bind the world.

"Some of us, of course, possess a grandiloquence, and around such folk the world is more labile, more agreeable to persuasion."

The Lady's bright eyes flicked to me. "Oliver," she said charming and disturbing me with such familiarity, "how would you rate your Master at such talk?"

"He is the most powerful speaker there ever was, Marm."

The Lady's eyes narrowed, her lips grew tight with mischief.

Something the Master did not notice, being an altogether serious man.

"It is a miserable day out, Mr Collins. Why don't you make it a fine one?"

My Master, surprised by this, brought a finger to his lips, then gave a hesitant smile. it was Thursday, after all, at last, though, he nodded.

"Very well," he said, then true to his word, his spoke the day into one of sunshine, and birdsong, a gentle breeze lifted the curtains and tugged at the Lady's hair.

She laughed with pleasure at this simple-to-him, though wondrous-to-her, display, and they spent the rest of the day in the garden. Much to the delight of her many pets, which though at first surprised, were quick to shake away their rainy day stupors, and set the air alive with barks and quacks, and mark the Master's pants with muddy paws.

All the way home, Collins sat in the cabin of our carriage, his face flushed and I knew for certain that he was in love, just as I knew that the Lady was not.

The next time he visited her, she appeared embarrassed and it did not take long for the reason to reveal itself.

"I must apologise," she said. "I did not mean to make you do it."

He frowned at her. "Do what, my dear?"

"Change the weather. The papers have been up in arms about it all week."

"Oh, *that*," Collins said. "It was nothing. I've always found Thursday, rain day, to be annoyingly arbitrary."

Of course, he had not been so casual or dismissive to the half dozen raging parliamentarians who'd come a visiting Thursday evening.

"Let's not speak of it again."

Three more times he visited her and though every time she was polite and engaging, he did not pierce the edge of reserve that surrounded her.

They spoke of the Grammar, of its potency, of the ways it had been used throughout its short history and the ways it had been undone, for Eloquence and Colloquy are back-and-forth things for both good and ill.

And, on the third visit, he got down on one knee, reached into his pocket for the ring we had talked into being just that morning, and declared his love for her.

At which she shook her head and looked deflated as though the worst of her fears had come true—for she must have suspected it was coming. "Though I would wish it otherwise, Mr Collins, I cannot love you, for all your sweet talk and good company."

And at once I knew why, though Master could not. He blinked and balanced on his knee like a puppy slapped in the face.

"I do not understand," he said. "I would shape the world for you. All my eloquence is yours."

"Exactly," she said. "How might I really know you love me? How would I know that you did not merely speak it? No, I could not trust such a glorious speaker. For all that it may be to my benefit, I cannot marry you, Sir."

My Master got to his feet and dipped his head, his eyes never leaving hers. "Then let me bid you a fond farewell—though I I suspect you may look upon even that with wariness—and beg of you forgiveness for the discomfort that I have caused you."

With that we were out the room and into his carriage and away. We did not speak for some time, he too angry to open his mouth, and me too frightened to disturb the silence. In moments like that you never know what words might turn up. In moments like that it is far better not to find out.

Eloquence is not about intellect. Errant words are the

problem of our age. Talk is cheap, but oh so potent. Novelists are dangerous; their imaginings could sweep across the land in clouds of drama and inference, *and* Historians, revisionists or not, were far too potent . . . so was best that they were purged. Only the lexicon remains.

Which is why the Grammar is not taught to all but those deemed fit and proper for Parliament, and the tongues of the seditious—or those that seem far too good at speech and far too common—cut out.

On our way home, we passed the most popular pubs. *The Stilled Tongue, The Looker* and *The Taciturn Arms* and not one did the Master wish to visit.

Finally he did speak, regarding me with his wounded eyes. "Most unexpected was it not? Most unexpected."

Oh, after that he strode about the house, a raging melancholic. He told the sky to rain and was met with a downpour. Collins had few friends and it had always been thus. Small talk made him uneasy. After all, he wielded the Biggest talk, the most meaningful. Everyday words, every day constructions were as difficult to him as the Grammar was to most common folk.

For five days, he kept to himself, barely touched his food, for all that I begged him to. Hardly made a mess, just sat, drank far too much and whispered to himself. I thought he'd lost his mind, or at the very least his wit, when he came at me from his rooms a wild smile stretched across his face.

"I know what I must do," he said. "Fetch my driver, I have to see her again."

* * *

"Please, it saddens me to see you this way," the Lady said. "And if your intent is the opposite, and you are striving to lift my spirits at the sight of you then you have failed."

"Then let me woo you."

The Lady lowered her eyes, then applied their weight anew upon his desperate face.

"If you feel you must then yes. But I have one request just one and you must give me your word."

And even Collins could see where this was going.

"I would not use my words to change you," he said. "I will not woo you that way. I will not speak you to love, merely show you mine."

"You give me your word."

"I give you my word."

* * *

And with that word it began. Such a wooing as the world had never seen before.

He cast the most wondrous nets, shaped earth and sky to her snaring and all that potency was nothing to a single no from her lips. He unknitted histories and she bound them up again. He charged the air with poetries as controlled and wild as sonnets, made rondels of the heavens. He cried out her beauty like the night, made cloudless days, or set rain to fall if she said that was what might make her happy—and the Lady was fond of ducks and the sanguine creak of frogs, so she was of a mind to appreciate rain as well as clear skies.

He would pour over the Lexicon at night, muttering to himself, studying as closely as he ever had the Grammar.

"We've a most inelegant reality, even if it is an eloquent one," My Master said his face tight with the frustrations of affection unreturned; of pleasantries pleasant enough, but not the passionate things for which he yearned.

So often did he attend her that he began to neglect his civic duties. No longer could you be certain it would rain on Thursday because she might not wish it. Sombre Mitreday might grow all carnival with elephants and ribbons and musicians and wiry balloons. And the people on the street might look at each other and nod, "Why it's master Collins gone all in love with the Lady."

And this went on for months for there was no one to challenge him, no one he could not drown out. Though several tried and suffered for it—none too badly—he was a man possessed with love not villainy.

"He'll have us all as rabbits singing for his mistresses pleasure," other, weaker speakers in Parliament might whisper to me, knowing I had his ear a little and I would nod my head, because it was true and I had nary an inkling where it might end.

* * *

The Lady's favourite duck died and My Master spoke to Death, talked it into his Great hall and talked it out of taking the duck.

He took the returned-to-living thing, its duck eyes blinking, to the Lady.

The Lady frowned. "Mr Collins, I am indeed rather fond of ducks, and Puddleson Dickens the third more than most, but am also fond of a roast and you've done my kitchen no courtesy."

In a fit of petulance, he wrung poor Puddleson's neck then and there.

"It's one or the other for you, isn't it?" the Lady said. "You don't understand the muddiness of words, their glorious multiplicities. Precision isn't everything, you know."

He lay the duck down on the table. "Precision is everything."

* * *

"Love, it is a word that will not bend to my will," my Master said, and mumbled under his breath. "Why won't it bend to my will? How might I persuade it?"

But he did not understand that love is its own Grammar, its own singular persuasion more potent than a thousand parliaments.

He did not understand that love is not power, love is its opposite.

* * *

And even I was surprised at last when the wooing was done, and he sat with the Lady and, holding her hands, asked again that she might marry him. The Lady's face reddened and she looked away, then back into his eyes.

"I am so sorry, James," she said. "But still I cannot say yes."

"But have I not made the world abundant with wonders? Haven't I shaped the very clouds, diverted rivers, raised monuments and challenged death for you?"

"And, yet again, that is why I must say no. I cannot love you truly, when the world is so mutable to your tongue. I cannot love you and be me. For all that I admire you, for all that I respect you, I still cannot love you."

He paled. "Then there is one thing left to me," he said, rising to his feet. "One final persuasion and then I will ask you again."

He dipped his head. "I may be gone a while, but I will return."

* * *

And so he undid.

He shouted down the Grammar, unmade its potency, as best he could, because words could always shape thoughts, but words alone would never again remake reality. So eloquent was he in this task that it took him but four months to fulfil it. And when he was done, he knew it could not be unspoken, he knew he had changed the world forever, that the Underlying Mechanism of the Bottle Grande would never listen so attentively again.

And he was not the only one. Parliamentarians lined our hall.

"What have you done?" they demanded, though they already knew. "The world is ruined," they said. "Talked out."

The Master shook his head. "The world will run as it ran before. Dear sirs, talk is still not cheap. And there will be other duties to which we must attend."

One man made to strike him and, out of habit, the Master tried to whisper it away. The fist struck him hard, then another and another.

But none of these men where used to fighting. I pulled them from my poor master and pushed them from the house. I knew how to fight.

The Master looked at me with a new respect. "You'll have to teach me that," he said.

"With pleasure," I said, thinking of the occasional bloody nose I might administer myself, still smarting over Death's visit to the house.

* * *

Hoarse and bleeding, and with me to hold him up, he took his carriage along the thoroughfare and down to her residence.

"The World is ruined," he whispered.

And all the way I sat and watched this world remade, this sticks and stones world, where words could sting but no longer hurt. This world where tongues might wag again now the Grammar was gone.

"The World is ruined," he whispered again.

But it was not.

* * *

He struck his hand against the door, his knuckles bleeding. The sound so feeble because he was so feeble, but still someone came to the door, then led him in to the Lady's drawing room.

And when she entered, the room lit up with a magic that was beyond words, doubly beyond words now. At the sight of him, she hurried to his side.

"It is done," he said, hoarse and broken. She rubbed his face and my master winced.

"Come outside," he said. "Into the garden."

We all did.

"Can't you feel it?" he said.

"Feel what?" the lady asked.

"The Bottle Grande, the air, the soil, it's no longer listening."

I smiled. He was right, everything was as it was, but indifferent. The world did not strain to hear, nor hang upon our every word, it just existed.

"You did this for me?"

"And you alone," the Master said. "All done because I love you, love you more than words can ever express. And because of such a love I have bound this world up, imprisoned it. Oh, but I am a fool."

"Fool you are, but you have not bound up this world, just freed it, as you have freed my heart," the Lady said, and clutched his hands close to her breast.

"Freed it? I do not see what you mean . . . "

"Would you just shut up," the Lady said, "and kiss me?"

And that, words fled, is what my Master did.

PUBLICATION HISTORY

"Threnody," first appeared in *Eidolon* 15, 1994.

"Always," first appeared in *Fables & Reflections*, 2004.

"Bounty," first appeared in *Deep Outside,* 2001.

"Drift," first appeared in *Vernacular* 1, 2000.

"To End All," first appeared in *Antipodean Science Fiction* 37, 2001.

"Naked," first appeared in *Altair* 4, 1999.

"Tar Baby," first appeared in *Agog Fantastic Fiction,* 2002.

"Carousel," first appeared in *Aurealis* 25, 1999.

"A Woman in a Pool of Light In a Quantam Universe Smokes a Cigarette,," first appeared in *Vernacular* 2, 2001.

"Clockwork," first appeared in *Glimpses*, 2003.

"Girl in a Black Dress," first appeared in *Antipodean Science Fiction* 42, 2001.

"Sisyphus Drinking," first appeared in *Vernacular* 4, 2002.

"Wind Down," first appeared in *Aurealis* 30, 2002.

"A Thief is a King in the Halls of the Night," first appeared in *Australien Absurdities*, 2002.

"My Brother is God," first appeared in *Borderlands* 2, 2003.

"Will and His Lady Luck," first appeared in *Antipodean Science Fiction* 66, 2003.

"Looking Back," first appeared in *Fables and Reflections* 1, 2002.

"Endure," first appeared in *Agog Smashing Stories*, 2004.

"Commuter," first appeared in *Redsine Online*, 2000.

"Anabiosis," first appeared in *Ticonderoga Online*, 2004.

"Don't Got No Wings," first appeared in *Encounters*, 2004.

"Porcelain Salli," first appeared in *Aurealis* 2004.

"Persuasion," is original to this collection.

www.ingramcontent.com/pod-product-compliance
Lightning Source LLC
Chambersburg PA
CBHW022145050726
47590CB00002B/587